The Deadly
Chase

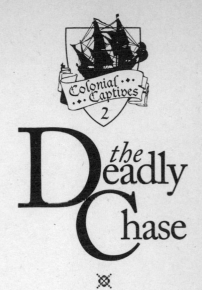

the Deadly Chase

ANGELA ELWELL HUNT

Tyndale House
Publishers, Inc.
WHEATON
ILLINOIS

Library of Congress Cataloging-in-Publication Data

Hunt, Angela Elwell, date–
    The deadly chase / Angela Elwell Hunt.
       p. cm. — (Colonial captives ; bk. 2)
      Summary: While continuing her voyage to America, Kimberly encounters not only a
deaf girl who attempts to save a baby whale but also a Jewish boy who accepts Christ.
    ISBN 0-8423-0330-8 (pbk.)
    [1. Voyages and travels—Fiction. 2. Whaling—Fiction. 3. Christian life—Fiction.]
    I. Title II. Series: Hunt, Angela Elwell, date– Colonial captives ; bk. 2.
PZ7.H9115De 1996
[Fic]—dc20   95-47926

Printed in the United States of America

02   01   00   99   98   97   96
9   8   7   6   5   4   3   2   1

Happy are those who mourn,
for they will be comforted.

* * *

With thanks to
Dr. Sandy Epstein

GLOSSARIES

Parts of a Ship:
aft: behind; toward the stern
bilge: the low point of a ship's hull
bow: the forward part of the ship
bowsprit: a rod extending forward from the bow out over the
 water
clumsycleat: a cutout in a strip of wood to brace the harpooner's
 knee and prevent slipping
companionway: a narrow stairway leading from deck to deck
deck: the floor
fore: ahead; toward the bow
hold: a cargo area below deck within the ship's hull
mainmast: the largest, center mast on a ship
mainsail: the largest sail on the mainmast
mizzenmast: the mast nearest the stern
orlop deck: the lowest deck of a ship with four decks
port: the left side of the vessel, as one stands on a ship and faces
 the bow
starboard: the right side of the vessel, as one stands on a ship and
 faces the bow
stern: the rear of the ship
thwart: a rower's seat extending across a boat
topgallant: a relatively small sail high on the mast
yard: a long, slender rod fastened horizontally across the mast to
 support a sail
yardarm: either half of a yard

Sailors' Terms:

aboard: on board a vessel

aground: snagged on shore or bottom of waterway

ahoy: call to attention

ballast: heavy objects used to maintain the ship at the proper draft

bilge rats (slang): boys who work below deck; also called bilge boys

bosun: foreman; officer in charge of the crew

captain: officer who is master or commander of the ship

caravel: Portuguese ship with square sails on her bowsprit and front mast, but lateen (triangular) sails on her other three masts

clear the decks: all idle crew must go below

draft: how far down in the water a ship is

even keel: condition of floating properly upright in water

furl: roll up or take in sails

make sail: raise sails and set out

pilot: officer who steers the ship in and out of harbor

reefed sail: a sail partly lowered and secured

remora: a sucking fish about eight inches long that is common in the Mediterranean. The fish attaches itself to flat surfaces and can only be dislodged with difficulty.

squall: a sudden, intense storm at sea

Other Words:

bodice: the upper portion of a woman's dress

breeches (pronounced "britches"): knee-length trousers

indentured servant: one who agrees to be purchased as a servant for an agreed-upon term of years, usually to pay off a debt for sea passage

kirtle: a woman's skirt

knave: a rascal; a false, deceitful person

save: often used in the seventeenth century to mean "except"

sea biscuit: a large, coarse, hard, unleavened bread; also called hardtack

sempstress: a seamstress; dressmaker

victuals (pronounced "vitt-els"): stored provisions or food

INTRODUCTION

"In 1627, 1,500 kidnapped children arrived in Virginia. They came from Europe and some became great successes. A six-year-old, kidnapped by a sailor and sold in America, married his master's daughter, inherited his fortune, and bought the sailor, by then a prisoner."
—*The Encyclopedia of American Facts and Dates*

The story so far . . .
In May 1627, Mistress Mary Hollis of London received a letter from across the sea. Her husband, who had served seven years of indentured service in the English colony at Jamestown, wrote to ask his wife and daughter to join him in Virginia. Despite her failing health, Mary and her fourteen-year-old daughter, Kimberly, sold all the family's possessions in London and booked passage upon a ship, the *Seven Brothers*, which was due to sail for Jamestown.

After boarding, Kimberly and her mother found themselves in a passenger hold filled with over one hundred captured children who were to be sold in Virginia as indentured servants. They had no choice but to join the others and make the best of a long and difficult journey across the great western ocean.

After only a few days at sea, Kimberly's mother died from phthisis, the disease we know as tuberculosis. Kimberly must now face the journey alone but for the friends she has made aboard the ship and her faith in God.

WEEK THREE

Wednesday, May 26, 1627

1

An air current brought the promise of dawn into the crowded hold below the main deck, and Kimberly Hollis sat up, unable to sleep. This was one of those rare moments when all 124 inhabitants of the *Seven Brothers* were silent, and Kimberly smiled, happy to discover a quiet interval in which she could think without being peppered with questions or comments from the children with whom she sailed.

The adventure of the past week had faded to memory in the last two days, and no one aboard the *Seven Brothers* had seen any sign of the fierce pirate Delmar de Chavez. He and his dark ship had vanished from the horizon in a strange and powerful whirlwind, and Kimberly and the others could not forget that God had miraculously delivered them from the wide mouths of the pirate's cannon and certain destruction. Thatcher, who had particularly good reasons to fear the pirate, was especially glad that the swarthy sea rover had not caught up to threaten the *Seven Brothers* again.

In the days following the strange phenomenon at sea, Kimberly had tried to restore some sort of order to the chaos on the children's deck. Captain Blade was as adamant as ever that the children should remain below and out of sight. Though Kimberly often begged Squeege, the bosun, to allow the children a breath of fresh air on the upper deck, he insisted that the captain had good reasons for keeping the children below.

And so, trapped like mice in a basket, the captive children lived and slept and tried to entertain themselves on the long journey across the great western ocean to Jamestown, Virginia. They had been at sea for two weeks, and in that time Kimberly had learned to admire and appreciate many of the others for their special abilities and gifts. Wingate Winslow, an all-around pleasant and good-natured orphan boy, was probably her best friend and confidant. Brooke Burdon, a vain and somewhat spoiled girl who had been kidnapped while momentarily out of the care of her nanny, seemed to grow more gentle every day and delighted in teaching English to the two French twins, Denni and Daryl. After two weeks of hard life at sea, Brooke was a far different girl from the one who threw loud and fierce temper tantrums in her first days aboard the *Seven Brothers*.

Abigail O'Brien had never thrown a temper tantrum, for she could not speak, and Kimberly often looked at the pretty red-haired girl and wondered what thoughts went through her mind. She was probably thirteen or fourteen, but seemed much older than her years. She could write well enough to give the others her name, but her real skill lay in her ability as a sempstress. She had never shared the story of how she came to be aboard the kidnappers' ship, but Kimberly suspected that someone had seen Abigail's fine needlework and hoped to sell her for a high price in the Virginia colony. But though her needle flashed with artistry and her face was an open canvas upon which they could read her emotions, since the first day of the voyage Abigail had not uttered one word or sound.

Christian, the blind boy who used to beg for pennies on the streets of London, sang more sweetly than anyone Kimberly had ever heard, and even the reserved and stern Captain Blade had taken to calling Christian to the upper deck so the seamen might enjoy a song or two. It wasn't as though the sailors never heard music; the air was routinely filled with their hoarse voices singing their rough sea chanties as they worked to haul sail and trim the ropes. But Christian's singing was sweet and powerful. Squeege said even the creatures of the deep stopped to listen when Christian's pure voice lifted over the dark, blue waters.

Christian was not the only singer aboard ship. While he happily sang for others, Ethan Reis sang only for himself and occasionally for Kimberly. Ethan was Jewish, the only Jew Kimberly had ever known, and his bittersweet songs in a lilting foreign tongue seemed to answer a yearning call of Kimberly's heart. Her mother had died not many days past, and Ethan's songs seemed to give voice to the pain in Kimberly's soul. Though she knew her mother would not want her to mourn, Kimberly could not help missing her.

As she quietly grieved, Kimberly thought a lot about the father she hadn't seen in seven years. Thomas Hollis had left England when Kimberly was only seven years old, and he had spent the last seven years working as an indentured servant in the harsh colony of Jamestown. Her mother had often said that it was a miracle he had survived the disease and rough conditions of that colony, and that it was God's will that she and Kimberly set sail to join him for a new life in the land called America.

Now her father was a free man, and he waited in Jamestown for his wife and daughter. It would be Kim-

5

berly's job to tell him that his beloved wife—her mother—waited for them both in heaven.

The faint beginnings of day pinked the sky on the eastern horizon, and Kimberly lay back down and turned onto her side to study the clouds visible through the three open windows in the starboard side of the children's hold. The violet sky was filling with gold radiance as the sun rose, unmarred by the movements of a single bird. They were alone on the ocean, too far out to sea for the companionship even of the far-flying gulls.

In the quiet of morning, Kimberly felt lonely. Since her mother's death she had assumed the role of leader and teacher of the other children, and that role somehow set her apart. She and her mother had been the only paying passengers in the cargo hold of the *Seven Brothers*, and Kimberly was the only child aboard who was not destined to be sold into indentured service once the ship reached Jamestown. She would meet her father, and they would begin a new life, but she felt a certain responsibility for the others. Her mother had believed that God had brought them to this particular ship to help the frightened, frantic captive children, and now Kimberly tried to fill her mother's role and help the others prepare for the life that would be theirs when they arrived at the colony.

Someone stirred in the gloom of the hold, and Kimberly felt a tug on her kirtle. Reluctantly turning her eyes from the brightening window, she saw Thatcher Butler crouching near her. "Good. I thought you were awake," he whispered, his rough voice grating through the stillness like a rusty hinge. "I've an idea about what I can do to help the younger ones."

"Can't it wait until later?" Kimberly whispered, turning back toward the window. She wasn't in the mood to listen to Thatcher's enthusiastic ideas. Last week he'd been sullen and unwilling to help her do anything, but since their miraculous rescue from the pirates, Thatcher

6

had been a changed boy. Now he was eager, even desperate, to help Kimberly direct the younger children.

"Nay, it won't take but a minute," Thatcher went on, seeming not to notice that she didn't want to talk. "You said we've got to help the others survive in Jamestown, right? Well, I survived, and mighty well, too, on the streets of London, and I've gleaned a skill or two. I thought I could teach the boys how to cut purses. 'Tis not glamorous work, to be sure, but if a body's hungry and needs to eat, cutting purses will get him fed—"

"Cutting purses?" Kimberly said as she turned to scowl at him, irritation edging her voice. "Stealing? Have you lost your mind, Thatcher? We'll not teach anyone how to steal, but how to make a good and honest living."

Thatcher's face fell, and Kimberly could almost hear her mother's gentle voice chiding her. It was obvious he wanted to help, and a life of petty crime was all he had known in England. Perhaps she had been too hard on him, but she was still sleepy and wanted a few more moments of silence for herself.

"We'll not steal, but you can teach them something else," she amended, softening her voice. "Leave me, Thatcher, until the sun is well up, and then we'll talk again. But I appreciate your willingness to help."

Thatcher's handsome face cleared as he nodded and moved away, and Kimberly sighed as she turned back to the window. Keeping everyone happy and content was hard work. She hoped she had the strength to last the voyage.

* * *

While they were eating dinner below on the ship's third deck, Squeege announced that Abigail, Wingate, and two younger boys were to be put to work with thread and canvas. Abigail felt her heart turn over in pleased surprise when the bosun gestured for the foursome to follow him to the upper deck.

She paused for a moment on the sailors' deck and closed her eyes to breathe deeply. The warm afternoon air, bathed in sunlight, carried faint hints of coming summer days. Though the wide windows in the children's hold offered a fair amount of ventilation, still the odors of the privy and the stale smell of unwashed bodies clung to everyone and everything. Up here, amid the sun and wind, the air was crisp and scented with the mist of spring.

"Over here, girl," Squeege called, and she opened her eyes and stepped nimbly over piles of rope and canvas. She could feel the eyes of the seamen on her as she followed Squeege and the boys, and she squared her shoulders as if to say that she would not be bothered by their curious stares. Very little bothered her. She had learned long ago it was best not to let anything touch her heart, mind, or soul.

"Now," Squeege said, settling himself upon a wooden cask and pulling a pile of canvas onto his lap. "A proper sailor cares for his sails far more than for his own skin. If the captain calls for the men to cast off the gaskets and gather the canvas, the men will do what he commands. But when the order comes to let fall, if the sheets are full of holes what good are they going to do a ship or her crew? A ship can't be spreading her wings if they're clipped, if ye take me meaning."

"So what you're saying," Wingate ventured, sitting cross-legged on the deck next to Squeege, "is that you want us to mend the sails."

Squeege nodded. "Of course. If we were a royal ship, say a ship in the king's navy, we'd have a master sailmaker on board and that would be his job. But since we're not, we pass the job around to any and all who will take it. And since young Kimberly said y'all are looking for things to do, and since the little miss here hath a talent with a needle and you didn't do a bad job before . . ."

Abigail reached out for a corner of the canvas and ran her palm over the fabric. It was rough beneath her hands and stiff with salt spray, but her sensitive fingers could feel the strength underneath the stiffness, the cords of hemp that had combined to create a fabric strong enough to propel a ship through a great ocean.

Squeege presented a wax-filled bullock's horn, and Abigail could see several iron needles that had been thrust into the wax. "I have all the tools ye need," Squeege said, respectfully nodding toward Abigail, then looking at the other children, who had not helped on the sails last week. "There's a braided tail of twine in my box, as well as a pricker for making holes in the canvas. The young miss will show ye what to do with these, and I'll be about my work."

Abigail glanced up at the snapping sails overhead. The sheets, as the seamen called them, were of simple design, with sharp creases in the edges of the canvas and ropes running through the hems. Unless these boys were complete butterfingers, she'd have them sewing neat and proper sails within the hour.

She gave Squeege a confident nod and smiled as relief flooded his face. "'Tis very good," he muttered, more to himself than to them. "The captain will be pleased that I haven't had to take men off the watch. Make me proud, lads and lassie, and I'll bring ye up here more often."

And that, Abigail thought as she felt the sun warm her face, *would be worth any amount of work*. She immediately plucked one of the needles from the bullock's horn and held it up to demonstrate the proper way to thread a needle.

9

2

As she stitched in the haze of the afternoon sun, Abigail's mind went back, picking up the strings of time. *"Abigail, me darlin', you must sew a straight line, and never make less than eight stitches in the distance from your thumb knuckle to nail,"* a voice rang in her memory. She was a small child again, sitting at the knee of a pretty red-haired Irish girl who fussed and scolded every time Abigail made a sound.

"If the mistress is to keep us on, we can't be a bother to her," the girl said, brushing a stray strand of hair from her face. "Now, Abby, sew this seam again, and be quick and silent about it. Mistress Ludlow can't abide the sight and sound of me pattering about, and if you add to the noise in the house . . ."

The unspoken threat hung in the air, and Abigail shrank back and made a conscious effort to lessen the sound of her breathing. She did everything quietly. She did not speak, or laugh, or cry, or sing. She never wore shoes in the house, not even on the coldest days, lest the sound of her wooden soles disturb the mistress. For as long as she could remember, she had been told not to make noise, and now silence was a part of her nature. Endlessly, always, she was told to be quick and quiet.

Her fingers trembled as she sewed the seam. If she did not do it correctly, the red-haired girl might send her away. Where would she go if she were forbidden to sleep in her small cupboard? What would she eat if the girl refused to share her dinner plate?

"Lizabeth!"

The sharp cry echoed from the mistress's quarters, and the young girl jerked in alarm at the sound. With a guilty glance toward Abigail, the girl lay her finger across her lips, then slipped from her stool. "Coming, ma'am," she called, rushing from the room.

Abigail bent forward and stitched more quickly. She heard Lizabeth cry, "But Mistress Ludlow! Where will I go?"

The lady's reply was muffled. Abigail's hand slipped, and the needle bit deep into her index finger. She stuck her bleeding finger into her mouth and listened intently for another sound from the mistress's chamber.

But none came. Lizabeth had been removed from the house. Abigail felt a trembling rise from her stomach. Before she realized it, her entire form quaked with a new kind of fear that twisted her face and shook her body from toe to hair. Despite her quivering hands, she finished the seam she had been sewing, then crept to the cupboard where Lizabeth had always hidden her. After curling up inside, she closed the door.

She waited inside the cupboard for two days before anyone found her. Limp from hunger and thirst, Abigail blinked when a scullery maid threw the cupboard doors open. Terror stole her breath when the maid covered her face and screamed, then a host of servants came running.

"What the devil?"

"Where'd *that* come from?"

"Whose child is she?"

"Do you think the girl Lizabeth—"

"She's all of four years old, don't ye think?"

"Just wait until the mistress hears of this!"

"Quiet! A sick woman lies in here!"

The bellowing roar from the mistress's bedchamber interrupted the servants' discussion. Undaunted, they dropped their voices to a whisper as they began to question Abigail. They asked her name, where she had come from, and why she had hidden in the cupboard. Abigail had neither answers nor the voice with which to talk to them. She had always lived there, had always slept in the cupboard, had always been told to remain silent. Their questions did nothing to calm the fear that spurred her heart to beat unevenly. Their demands that she speak only strengthened her resolve to remain silent.

At length she was taken to Mistress Ludlow. The wealthy and fashionably feeble mistress sat up in her bed and looked down her thin nose toward Abigail. "She does not speak?"

"Not a word," the steward said. "Nor a sound."

The mistress nodded knowingly. "The child is an idiot; anyone can see that. Can she do anything at all?"

"She's little more than a baby," the cook interjected.

"She ought to go to an orphanage," the scullery maid proposed.

"She may have an aptitude for tailoring," the steward pointed out. "Lizabeth was very skilled with a needle."

"Not skilled enough," the mistress snapped. "The bodice of my last gown was too tight and caused me no end of discomfort. 'Tis unbearable enough that I am scarcely able to draw breath because of my weakened condition, but to have matters complicated by a too-tight bodice—"

"'Twas a terrible mistake, and you were right to send her away," the steward said soothingly. "But surely this little one had no fault in the matter. Why don't you keep her here and see if she might not please you? 'Twould be a hard thing to send a child of such tender age into the world alone."

"Would keeping her be better than selling her to the sempstress?" Mistress Ludlow asked, her jeweled hand flashing against the bedcovers.

"Much better," the steward answered, bowing his head respectfully. "You could train her to sew as you please. And you can see that she is already as silent as a butterfly."

Mistress Ludlow's thin eyes narrowed as she considered the child before her, and Abigail stood motionless before that harsh gaze, as though she were fastened to the wall of the lady's bedchamber.

"So be it," the lady finally said, waving her hand toward the steward. "But you are responsible for her care and keeping. I never want to see her unless I call for her, and I do not want to be reminded of her presence. 'Tis troubling enough to think that I have housed and fed a child without knowing that I was housing and feeding it—"

"Never fear, my lady," the steward said, pressing his hand on Abigail's shoulder as he propelled her from the room. "You will not regret this decision."

The pressure of the steward's hand had been as warm as this May sunshine on her shoulder, and it was with an effort that Abigail shook herself out of the memory. She had remained in Mistress Ludlow's house for nearly ten more years, until the kind steward died and Mistress Ludlow made good on her intention to sell Abigail to the sempstress. The mistress, now truly too ill to have much need for ball gowns and court dresses, sent Abigail away the morning after the steward's burial. But the men paid to escort her to the sempstress's shop took

Abigail to the dockyard on the River Thames instead. With money from the sempstress in their pockets and additional money from the colonial kidnappers, the crooked escorts left Abigail aboard the *Seven Brothers* and told the captain that her talent with a needle would bring a generous price in the Virginia colony.

If her kidnappers thought Abigail would be upset or disappointed at the unexpected turn of events, they were wrong. She accepted this situation as she accepted everything life brought her way—without comment or complaint. It was a relief to be out of Mistress Ludlow's stern household, and Abigail knew nothing of sempstresses' shops. But she was pleased to hear that she would be sewing, for in needlework she had found a way to escape her uneventful, unloved life. The threads were a melody, the fabric chords of harmony, and when they joined together under the careful conducting of her flashing needle, she created designs and textures that sang, intricate symphonies only she could hear and enjoy.

This was the best way she could express herself. Abigail O'Brien had been silent for so long, she had no idea how to speak. And now that she was free from the code of silence that had dominated Mistress Ludlow's household, she was too embarrassed to open her mouth and try.

* * *

The children aboard the *Seven Brothers* seemed to wilt like hothouse flowers as the sun set. By the time the last red rays were gleaming across the western waters, most of the captives were quiet and still as they lay on the hard wooden planking, waiting for sleep. Before she found a spot to lie down, Kimberly looked around the hold, mentally checking to see that all was well with the children she now saw as her responsibility. The young ones had been boisterous and hard to control this morning as she tried to teach the alphabet, and more than once she had come close to losing her temper with them. They wanted to play more than they wanted to learn, but Kimberly knew their lives would soon depend upon their willingness and ability to perform certain tasks in the Virginia colony.

They were stubborn and childish, and they had exhausted her, but now their eyes were heavy and ready for sleep, their grubby faces lined with weariness. Kimberly sank down onto the floor near the window and lay back, pillowing her head on her hands.

"How about a story, Kimberly?" Thatcher called from across the hold. "Something good."

"I'm too tired," Kimberly answered, yawning. "Can't someone else tell a story?"

"You tell the best ones," Wingate inserted loyally. "But mayhap I can think of one—"

"I know a story," Brooke called. Her blonde head popped up from the center of the hold, where she'd been lying down. "'Tis a good one, too. The groom from our stable used to tell it."

"If this is going to be another story about how rich you were," Thatcher called, his voice dry, "I don't want to hear it."

Brooke's lower lip edged forward in a pout. "'Tis no such thing. Do you want to hear it or not?"

"Tell it," Wingate said, leaning forward on his elbows. "I can't think of anything."

"All right." Brooke's plump face pinked in pleasure, and she clasped her hands together. "Our groom knew a man who served upon one of Sir Walter Raleigh's ships. Well, this man's ship was caught in a storm and the boat went down and everyone perished, except the man who knew our groom."

"What was his name?" Wingate called through the

gathering darkness. "The story will be better if you tell us his name."

Brooke frowned. "I don't know it."

"Make something up," Ethan said, propping his head on his hand. "The story won't change if you give him a made-up name, will it?"

"Nay," Brooke said. Her face brightened. "All right, then. His name was Clarence Gifford. Anyway, Clarence stayed afloat in one of the ship's shallops, but after five days and nights without water, he was near to death. He lay in the boat, ready to die, and prayed that the angels would come and escort him to heaven."

The air in the hold vibrated softly with the eternal whispers of the water outside, and a stillness settled upon the children. Brooke paused, and Kimberly noticed that no one dared to interrupt now. Every eye in the room was trained on Brooke, and the faces that had been heavy with exhaustion and sadness were now taut with attention. Perhaps this sea story was too near their own experience to be entertaining. If this story was likely to bring nightmares, maybe she should stop Brooke. But, like the others, Kimberly wanted to know what had happened to Clarence Gifford.

"The angels didn't come," Brooke went on, strengthening her voice as the air around them grew thick and close in the gathering darkness. "Someone else did. Clarence thought he heard singing, and he was sure 'twas the angels approaching, but then a dark man appeared from out of the sea and crawled into the shallop with him. The man's skin was green and covered with barnacles; his hair entangled with long strands of smelly seaweed—"

Several of the younger children began to whimper, and Kimberly sat up. "Brooke," she called, a warning note in her voice. "Is this story going to scare the little ones? Mayhap you shouldn't tell it, especially with darkness upon us."

"Well," Brooke said, twisting her hands. "Truth to tell, I'm beginning to frighten myself."

Wingate snorted. "You've got to have an ending. 'Tis not a proper story without a proper and true ending."

"All right," Brooke said, her voice growing higher in the dark. "Let's just say that another boat saw the shallop and rescued Clarence Gifford before the angels had a chance to carry him to heaven. And that's the end of the tale."

"A happy ending," Ethan said, rolling onto his back and folding his hands on his chest. "May the Master of the universe be praised."

"Amen," Kimberly said. She sighed and lay down for the night, but couldn't help but notice that several of the younger ones scooted closer to her before they settled down to sleep.

* * *

Abigail lay awake long after the others. The feel of a needle in her hands had brought back a flood of memories and questions that had haunted her for years. Who was she? Where did she come from? Everyone in Mistress Ludlow's household had assumed she was Lizabeth O'Brien's daughter, and no one had seen or heard from the Irish maid since the day Mistress Ludlow threw her out in a fit of temper.

But mayhap I am her sister, not her daughter, Abigail thought. *Mayhap she found me on a doorstep and took me home to care for me herself. And if, perchance, I am not Lizabeth's child, mayhap I am the true daughter of a lord or an earl or even the blessed king. For 'tis certain I was not born with a needle in my hands and a voiceless tongue in my mouth.*

The sounds of breathing children, creaking blocks, and straining rope filled her ears as troubling thoughts filled her head. But gently, persistently, a new sound intruded upon her mind, and the dark thoughts scattered as Abigail strained to hear and analyze the strangely melodic tones that echoed through the ship's hold. Was this the night cry of the green seaweed monster in Brooke's tale?

Abigail had rolled her eyes when Brooke told that silly story, but now she shivered. No one moved in the hold, and no footsteps pounded on the deck above. Was she the only one awake? Or was she the only soul aboard ship who could hear the strange melody?

She sat up in the darkness and stood to her shaky feet. With the ease of long practice, she moved as quietly as a ghost through the sleeping bodies and gazed out the window. The moonlit ocean stretched as far as she could see like a vast silvery blanket, but large patches of disturbed water mottled the flat swelling surface. If the sky had not been clear, Abigail would have sworn that rain fell upon those spots, but no clouds marred the moonlit sky. The mournful songs continued as she studied the troubled patches of water, and she was startled when several of them erupted with a flurry of movement that ceased as quickly as it had begun.

Her whole body tightened, then she took a slow breath. Suddenly Abigail wished with all her heart that she could speak. If she could, she would run up the companionway and ask Squeege or the captain what the strange movements of water were. There had to be a rational explanation, for green seaweed-haired men did not lurk beneath the surface to snatch people from ships.

From very near, a soft wail broke the silence. Abigail felt the noise pass through her, stir the air inside the ship, and raise the hair upon her arms. It was as if the sound had come from beneath the ship itself, but none of the others moved. If she alone could hear it, maybe the green man from Brooke's story was coming for her. . . .

A chilly dew formed on her skin as she clung to the railing of the window. She knew she should move away

19

from the water lest the green man rise up to snatch her, but her feet were frozen and would not obey her wishes.

A rotten stench brushed against her face and filled her nostrils, and Abigail opened her mouth in a silent gasp. Something huge moved in the water outside the window, and darkness itself pressed up through the velvet night and rose, dripping and dreadful, to stand before her. An ebony eye blinked and seemed to focus on her, then a series of rapid clicking sounds shrilled as the murky mass loomed toward her.

Abigail opened her mouth to scream, but no sound came forth. She covered her face with her hands as the waters parted a second time, and after a moment, when nothing happened, she peeked through her fingers. A second black shape, much smaller than the first, bobbed in the water outside the window. A distinct popping sound, like a sharp sneeze, broke the stillness, then the first black shape leaned as if to nudge the second, then slowly eased down into the water. The smaller shape answered with a gentle mewing sound, then disappeared into the deep.

Abigail stood motionless as the light of understanding dawned. *Whales!* A mother and her baby, no doubt, had just paid the ship a midnight visit, and she had been the only one to see them!

She leaned over the windowsill and scanned the silvery water, hoping for another glimpse of the pair. Suddenly the ocean was full of great black shapes that rolled and dove and swam lazily in the moonlight, chasing the small schools of fish that disturbed the water in flurries of excitement.

Come back, Abigail's heart cried out to them. *Please, I didn't know what you were!*

But though the sea churned for a few moments more before once again smoothing itself into a silvery mantle, the mother and her baby did not reappear.

3

"C*at*," Kimberly said, taking pains to write in big block letters on the wooden planks of the ship's flooring. The small lump of charcoal Wingate had found for her in the lower hold was difficult to grasp and hardly left any kind of mark at all on the darkened wood of the ship. But if the younger children were to learn to read and write, they would have to begin now and work hard.

"Do you see?" she said, turning to the dozen youngsters clustered around her feet. "*C-a-t* spells *cat.*"

"Meow," one of the boys called in a teasing voice.

Kimberly ignored his rude interruption and nodded eagerly. "That's right," she said. "Cat. Now the cat chases the *r-a-t*, the rat." As she turned to write the word on the floor beside her, the group broke into giggles. She whirled around in frustration. "What's so funny?" she demanded, planting her hands on her hips.

"Joshua crinkled his nose like a rat," one of the girls

volunteered, pointing to the mischievous boy who had meowed like a cat.

"Joshua, no more nonsense from you," Kimberly said, looking again at the floor. She swallowed her anger, but gripped the charcoal so tightly that her knuckles whitened. "You make an *r* like this, and you already know the *a* and *t.*"

One of the boys began to howl like a dog, and the girls giggled again. Kimberly turned and blazed at her students: "Why can't ye all be still and learn this? 'Tis important, ye know."

"I don't see why 'tis so important," Joshua said, thrusting his lower lip forward. "Me father never knew how to read nor write."

"Reading is more important than you can imagine," Kimberly said, crossing her arms. "If you know nothing when we arrive in Virginia, you'll be good for nothing but working in the tobacco fields. Do you want to sweat and strain out in the woods with the Indians and wild creatures and snakes? Or would you rather work in a house, with a kind master and mistress?"

The children looked round the circle with guilty faces, but not one of them had the courage to meet Kimberly's furious gaze. "Well," she went on, "you can't be a lady's maid or a steward unless you know how to cipher and read at least a little. I'm only doing this to save you from the fields, and if you knew what I know about Virginia, you'd be thanking me for my efforts!"

Ignoring Kimberly, Joshua of the cat and dog noises reached forward and yanked one of the girl's braids. "Ouch!" the girl yelped, reaching for her head, and another boy leapt to her defense and gave Joshua a swift kick.

Joshua stood to retaliate, and pandemonium broke loose. Screaming, the girls moved away from the brawling boys, and the other lads jumped into the fray with the

22

glee of children who have been cooped up for weeks and have finally found a way to cut loose and enjoy themselves. Half a dozen boys piled onto each other, pulling hair, punching, kicking, and squealing like pigs caught under a fence. Kimberly raised her hands helplessly and glanced around the hold to see who might come to her aid.

No one, it seemed, cared enough to even look up from their work. Brooke sat in a far corner with Denni and Daryl, deep in her efforts to teach English to the French twins, and Ethan sat at the far window murmuring one of his prayers. Wingate sat with Abigail and the other two boys assigned to repair the sails. From above, Christian's voice floated through the morning air in a song for the seamen. Thatcher, Kimberly knew, had finally been granted his wish to go up on deck and learn the art of sailing. He'd been badgering Captain Blade for such an opportunity since the beginning of the voyage, and today was his first chance to spend time with the sailors as they worked.

Which left Kimberly alone with her rambunctious students. "Stop it," she cried, stomping her foot on the deck as the free-for-all continued. "Stop hitting each other! Joshua! Colton! Get away from each other and mind your manners!"

No amount of threatening could lessen the boys' enthusiasm for the fight, and finally Kimberly walked to the edge of the tussling pile of lads and screamed as loud as she could: *"Stop fighting this instant!"*

Miraculously, every boy froze, eyes wide and mouths open. Kimberly reached into the mound of youngsters and grasped the shirt collars of the top two boys. "I will not tolerate this sort of behavior," she screamed, pulling the boys from the heap with all her might. "Do you think I am teaching you because I actually *want* to? Y'are more insane than that pirate de Chavez if ye truly think so. I'm teaching ye because 'tis for your own good, and yet not one of ye hath the good sense to listen to what I'm saying. Well, ye can all rot in those tobacco fields if you like, because if ye don't shape up and pay attention to me, that's where ye will be in two months. And if ye don't stop brawling like heathens and keep peace on this ship, I'll toss ye overboard myself."

She pulled two other boys to their feet, and the remaining two sat up, all traces of joy and merriment wiped from their faces. The six offenders regarded her with serious expressions, and Kimberly breathed a sigh of relief. She had completely lost her temper, but her outburst seemed to have worked, for not a sound could be heard in her section of the ship. Even the girls had stopped their giggling and were staring at her as seriously as if they were in church.

"We're sorry," Joshua breathed quietly, his hands folded in front of him, but Kimberly was in no mood for apologies.

"We'll see how sorry you are on the morrow," she said, turning on her heel. "For the rest of the day you can sit without me and study *cat* and *rat*. In the morning I'll expect you all to be able to write those words. But I'm tired of dealing with your foolishness."

In a flush of angry pride, she left her students and walked to the other side of the ship, as far away as she could possibly get without jumping into the sea. As she sat down and tucked her feet under her kirtle, twin voices of doubt and guilt began to argue in her brain. Was she wrong to have lost her temper? When they had first boarded the *Seven Brothers*, her mother had said it was God's purpose that they travel with these children so they could help them prepare for a new life in Virginia. Since her mother's death, Kimberly had tried to take her mother's place as a teacher and comforter, but how could a fourteen-year-old girl deal with the responsibility of all

24

these youngsters? They didn't want to listen to her, and they were too young to realize the differences and dangers of the American colony.

Her mind skated away from that unsolvable problem. For today, she'd let them think about how bad they'd been. And tomorrow, if she had to scream and yell to make them listen, she'd holler until she was hoarse. They just didn't seem to listen to her any other way.

* * *

Sitting by the window, a sheet of canvas in her lap, Abigail blocked the sounds and activity of the ship from her mind and concentrated her entire being upon listening for the low and lovely song of the whales. In the stark light of morning she had found it difficult to believe that she hadn't dreamed last night's encounter with the mother whale and her calf, but deep within her Abigail knew that the animals had somehow sought her out. An overpowering sense of awe filled her heart nearly to the point of bursting. Of all the people aboard ship, the whales had chosen her! They come up from their home in the deep and looked right at her, then they had serenaded her with their song.

As she lay awake and listened for the whales to return last night, Abigail had thought of proper names for her new friends. The mother whale she called Angel, like the angels in Brooke's story who were supposed to carry the sailor home to heaven. The baby she named Cailin, an Irish name meaning "little girl." (Abigail didn't know if the little whale was a girl, but she hoped she was.) Another whale had swum close to the mother and baby, a large and handsome creature Abigail called Ryan, or "little king." Several other whales appeared too quickly for Abigail to name them. But she hoped she'd see them again.

Now the sea seemed to be an enormous sheet of shin-

25

ing metal fading off into a blurred and distant horizon. In the distance, at a point before the place where the sea merged with the sky, a spout broke the surface of the deep. *A whale!* The evidence of the animal's presence momentarily made Abigail's breath leave her body and she froze, her hands poised over the canvas, her needle dangling in mid-air.

For the first time in her life, Abigail felt that she had truly communicated with someone. Last night the whales had somehow heard the cry of her heart as she lay lonely and awake in the bowels of the ship. And now the smiling creatures who sang the ocean to sleep were following at a safe distance. *Hello, my friends,* her heart called as she leaned forward toward the windows. *I wish I could swim with you. But I'm glad y'are following us.*

One hand spread the canvas and the other moved automatically, and, as her eyes continued to sweep the sea for another sign of the whales, her fingers began to embroider a perfect picture of the mother whale and her baby.

4

At midday the captain and his crew trooped down from above. After the bilge boys who lived in the belly of the ship had served the seamen, the children were allowed to venture into the lower hold and pick up their rations of one sea biscuit and a single cup of water.

Sitting on a barrel in the dim light of the lower hold, Kimberly gnawed on her biscuit without enthusiasm. Though she had not expected meals aboard ship to be either plentiful or delicious, since their encounter with the pirates the food had been meager and horrid. In order to escape the fierce sea rovers, Captain Blade had ordered his men to jettison several barrels of dried beef and other foodstuffs. Now one cup of water and one salty sea biscuit per day sustained everyone aboard ship. It was barely enough food to keep an invalid alive, and the vigorous appetites of the seamen and the growing children demanded more.

"I almost wish the pirates had taken our ship," Kimberly muttered to Wingate as she swallowed her last mouthful of dry biscuit. "Then at least we'd have something decent to eat."

"You can't mean that," Wingate protested, wiping crumbs from his chin. "Why, the pirates might have sunk us—and I'd rather be hungry than drowned."

"We'll all die of starvation if we have to live on this stuff for the rest of the voyage," Kimberly said. She licked a few remaining crumbs from her fingers, then wiped her hands on her kirtle. "We'll get sick, and the healthy ones will have to nurse those who are ailing. We've got to have fruit and meat if we're to stay healthy, Wingate. But where's the captain going to get what we need out here in the middle of the ocean?"

From far above, a distant voice shouted, "Sail ho!" Kimberly looked with surprise toward Wingate when she recognized the lookout's voice. It was Thatcher who had called out the warning.

"Is Thatcher still on the upper deck?" she asked, lifting an eyebrow. "I thought he'd be into trouble and locked below with the rest of us by now."

"Apparently the captain likes him," Wingate said, standing. He crinkled his brow as he moved toward the narrow ladder that led up to the children's hold. "I wonder if Thatcher's really seen a sail or if he's imagining things—"

Wingate was cut off by another, deeper voice. "Captain Blade! Sail ho, off the starboard bow!"

"There really is a ship!" Wingate said, turning to Kimberly. His eyes glowed with restless energy and fear. "Do you suppose that pirate—"

"Delmar de Chavez?" Kimberly asked, her voice squeaking. *Oh, dear God,* she prayed, *I really didn't mean it when I said I wished the pirates had taken us. Oh, please, Lord, don't let the sail belong to the pirates' black ship!*

Wingate scrambled up the ladder, and Kimberly followed after him as quickly as her legs could carry her.

* * *

From her spot at the window, Abigail heard the cry of "Sail ho!" and felt her heart begin to pound. If another ship approached, would the whales leave? She hardly had time to consider the thought before Kimberly, Wingate, Brooke, and Ethan crowded around her to stare at the sea beyond.

"'Tis a big ship," Ethan said, narrowing his eyes as he concentrated on the view beyond. "Not very much like the pirate ship, I think."

"The sails are definitely different," Brooke said, nodding her head. "The pirate ship had square sails on the front and triangular sails on the back, remember? Squeege said it was a caravan."

"A caravel," Kimberly corrected.

Abigail scanned the approaching ship carefully. The strange vessel was coming toward them with an impressive show of canvas, brilliant in the sun, and a white moustache of foam at her bow gave the impression that the ship traveled at great speed. It was a large craft, and from where she sat Abigail could see that the ship carried several small, narrow boats belly-up on her deck. This ship was definitely not the black caravel that Delmar de Chavez had commanded. So who were these men, and why were they approaching the *Seven Brothers?*

From the upper deck, the voices of Captain Blade and Squeege floated down through the open window. In such a small ship, Abigail reflected, any private remark passed on the deck was in truth a public statement. "Squeege, raise our colors," Captain Blade said, his voice clipped, and Squeege replied with another command to the sailor who manned the ropes. Abigail heard the creaking of cording and knew that the English flag was being

29

raised near the main mast. In answer, the approaching ship slowed her pace and responded by raising an identical flag.

"She's English," Brooke sighed in relief. "At least we won't be captured by the Spaniards."

"We're not out of danger yet," Wingate said, a warning note in his voice. "Have you forgotten that our Captain Blade and his men are kidnappers? If these Englishmen try to rescue us by taking the ship from the captain, they're likely to use their guns. The *Seven Brothers* may be sunk yet."

Abigail clenched her fists under the sheet of canvas in her lap. Why couldn't people leave them alone? She didn't want to be rescued and sent back to England! She wanted to remain where she was, on the ocean with the whales.

"Shh," Kimberly murmured absently, her eyes glued to the sight of the oncoming ship. "Listen."

The others fell silent and strained to hear Captain Blade's voice. "—must be cautious," he was saying, his voice more relaxed, "but if we befriend these seamen there's a chance they may trade or sell us the provisions we lack. Whalers are known to carry a generous supply of victuals."

Whalers! A sense of foreboding descended over Abigail with a shiver. These people were definitely not friends, for they had set out *intending* to kill and destroy.

"We'll send our shallop over to meet the captain and his crew," Captain Blade finished. "If all goes well, we'll ask for provisions and be well stocked on the morrow."

"Aye, Cap'n," Squeege answered, and as one the children lifted their eyes to the ship that approached behind a faint white edge of a lapping wave. When she was close enough for the children to see the face of her captain and crew, several of her sails were lowered, and the whaler came to a dead stop in the water. The two ships seemed to consider one another for a moment, then the shallop from the *Seven Brothers* splashed into the deep blue water. Armed with their muskets, Squeege and several seamen climbed down the rope and began to row the shallop toward the whalers' ship.

Abigail closed her eyes and sent a silent message: *If you can hear me, mama whale, stay away. This place is dangerous for you, Angel!*

* * *

While the other children slept around her, Kimberly sat at the window and watched the night clouds skip playfully across the full face of the moon. Up in the heavenlies a strong wind blew, but only the faintest of breezes moved across the surface of the ocean. Strangely enough, Captain Blade and Captain Moab, the master of the whaling ship, the *Orca Blue*, seemed not to care. Captain Moab sat now in Captain Blade's cabin as the two shared a jug of ale and stories of their days at sea.

Even from below Kimberly could hear the muffled sounds of their merrymaking. The two captains laughed and roared like long-lost friends, but Kimberly knew Captain Blade was trying to be friendly so he could win more supplies for his starving ship. She had no idea why Captain Moab would so readily agree to be entertained by a total stranger, but she prayed that Captain Blade's plan would provide the provisions they desperately needed.

The silvery ripples of the sea glistened in the moonlight, and Kimberly stretched her legs. She was bone tired from her long day and her frustration with the children. She knew she ought to lie down and sleep, but part of her felt like an anxious parent and wanted to stay awake until Captain Moab had left for his own ship and things were once again as they should be aboard the *Seven Brothers*. After so many days at sea in such a confined

31

space, the captives' ship had become a sort of community, and Kimberly knew that every soul aboard felt that something was out of place as long as a stranger remained among them.

At length she heard Captain Blade's vigorous voice cut through the air, and she knew the two men had come out of his cabin. "'Tis settled then," he said, his voice rumbling in the darkness. "Forty-eight casks of fruit and meat in exchange for forty-eight hours of manpower. My men, Captain, will be at your disposal come first light."

"I am pleased to hear it," Captain Moab answered, his words slightly slurred from the effects of the ale. "How fortunate that we found each other upon the sea. I, in need of men, and you, in need of victuals. We shall both help each other on the morrow and be the better for it, I think."

"Indeed we shall," Captain Blade answered, and then Kimberly heard the creaking of the ropes and heavy boots thudding against the side of the ship. Captain Moab was descending to the shallop that would escort him back to his own ship, and Squeege was doubtless going with him. She leaned out over the windowsill to make certain and saw the *Orca Blue's* captain. He was a short, plump man, about to burst the seams of his britches and the stitches of his shirt. But he climbed down the rope with an expert's grasp and strength and seated himself in the shallop with the air of a conquering king.

"Till the morrow, then," Moab cried, lifting an imaginary mug to salute Captain Blade. But there was no answer from the *Seven Brothers'* deck, and her bosun rowed the man away.

Kimberly waited until the shallop had crossed to the other ship, then she sighed and lay down upon the wooden planking. Her braid was a thick, lumpy cord that pressed uncomfortably against her back, and she sat up to loosen it. A sudden sniffing sound caught her attention. Looking around in the darkness, she saw a vague shape huddled on the narrow stairs leading to the upper deck. Red hair gleamed in the darkness. *Abigail? What is she doing awake at this hour?* Kimberly asked herself. *And why is she sad?* In all their days aboard ship, Kimberly had never known Abigail to be anything but easygoing and content.

"Abigail?" Kimberly called in a hoarse whisper. "Is anything amiss?"

She thought she saw Abigail shake her head, and as her eyes adjusted themselves to the dim light inside the hold she realized that the girl was furiously sewing in the dark. Curious, Kimberly crawled over the sleeping youngsters until she knelt by Abigail's side. Reaching out, she gingerly touched the strip of canvas in Abigail's lap, but the girl resisted and yanked the fabric away.

"I won't hurt it," Kimberly said, keeping her hand outstretched. "I just want to see what you're doing."

After a moment, Abigail relaxed and returned the canvas to her lap. Kimberly took hold of the fabric and lifted it into a shaft of moonlight. There, stitched in textures and shades so lifelike that the creatures seemed almost to swim on the canvas, was the perfect picture of two whales.

"How beautiful," Kimberly whispered, sensing that Abigail considered this work very precious and private. "But where did you ever see such a picture? In a book?"

Abigail shook her head, then pointed toward the window. Amazed, Kimberly followed her hand and realized in one heartbreaking moment that Abigail had seen whales in the waters where the whaling ship waited.

33

Friday, May 28

5

The song began slowly in the night, like a warm wind blowing underwater with soft moans. Abigail sat up in the darkness, instantly awake. A mewing wail came from one corner of the deep and was instantly answered by the reassuring sounds of the older whales as they whispered through the black waters. Abigail strained to hear more, and odd waterborne sounds came to her: distinct pops from the surface of the water, squeals, whistles, shrill chirps like birds, and slow, grating noises that reminded her of the snoring of the seamen above.

Slowly and deliberately, Abigail closed her eyes and used all her powers of concentration to tell the whales to go away. *'Tis not safe here*, she thought, clenching her fists as she tried to send her thoughts outward. *Why do you follow us? Why can't you understand what I'm trying to tell you?*

Still the assortment of sounds continued, and Abigail opened her eyes and sighed in frustration. She was only fooling herself. Why had she ever dared to imagine that she was special and that the whales could read her thoughts? They couldn't understand her. No one else could, either. The steward at Mistress Ludlow's house had always told Abigail to guard her thoughts, for God could hear them. "God knows the words you want to say and cannot," he told Abigail one afternoon when she was feeling depressed and lonely. "'For there is not a word in my tongue,'" he quoted from the Scriptures, "'but, lo, O Lord, thou knowest it altogether. . . . Whither shall I go from thy Spirit? or whither shall I flee from thy presence? . . . If I take the wings of the morning, and dwell in the uttermost parts of the sea; even there shall thy hand lead me, and thy right hand shall hold me. If I say, Surely the darkness shall cover me; even the night shall be light about me. Yea, the darkness hideth not from thee; but the night shineth as the day: the darkness and the light are both alike to thee.'

"You see, child," he had said, his hand falling upon her head, "God knows the words you want to say, and he will be with you always. Commit your ways and your life to him, and you will never find your life lacking for good things."

At the time Abigail had thought the steward a foolish, kindly old man who felt sorry for a motherless mute. Now she wished she had believed him. *'Twould be nice to know that God truly did hear my thoughts and would provide a way for the whales to escape.*

She rose to her feet and moved toward the window that faced away from the anchored *Orca Blue*, carefully stepping over the bodies of sleeping children. Leaning forward on the windowsill, she stretched her hand toward the surface of the water, wishing she could warn the whales away with a splash. But the water lay too far below the rim of the window, and if she leaned any further she would fall out.

36

She sank to her knees and rested her arms on the windowsill. If only she could swim! She'd never had an opportunity to try, and she didn't know if she could. One night she had heard the sailors debate the advantages and disadvantages of swimming. Some said swimming was good, for it was an exercise that brought pleasure, it was useful for carrying a line from one boat to another, and it could save a man's life if he fell into the sea. But others were equally convinced that swimming was a bad idea. Swimming, one sailor had argued, served only to prolong drowning in a shipwreck or if a man fell overboard. "If God had wanted us to be like the fishes," the man finished, "he'd have given us fins."

Abigail wished that she'd been born with fins. *At this moment,* she thought, watching the silk black water lap at the sides of the ship, *I'd give me very life to live in the water and be able to talk to the whales. Then I could warn them about the whalers, about the hunt that will begin at sunrise.*

A sour smell suddenly rose from the water, and Abigail crinkled her nose as she smiled in recognition. *The whales' breath!* In one fluid motion, not fifteen feet away from where she sat, a whale raised its bluntly rounded head out of the water and seemed to focus one of its great black eyes directly on her. She smiled in delight and leaned forward, not at all afraid, and then the waters parted again and the smaller head of the baby whale appeared. *Angel and Cailin!* The baby nuzzled its mother for a moment, then lowered its dark head into the water until only the blowhole was visible. While Abigail watched in fascination, the edges of the blowhole opened to the size of a teacup, then closed as the baby made a contented smacking sound.

Just like a kiss! Abigail thought. A puffing blast of breath further out on the waves caught her attention, and she looked beyond Angel and Cailin. The ocean outside her window now teemed with whales. A pod of at least fif-

37

teen moved in the waters, gently rolling upward for the life-giving air, then submerging again. Their massive heads threw no wake in the water, so smoothly did they move, and Abigail noticed that they seemed to swim by an up-and-down motion of their tails. Several swam upside-down with their flippers and chins out of the water as if they were relaxing, and Abigail bit her lip to stifle a giggle. They seemed so human!

Forgetting about sleep, she concentrated on watching the whales. Elegant and slim in the water, their tail fins were relatively small, and the rear of their bodies was narrow. Their side fins, or flippers, were sharply curved like the swords of Arab warriors in the east and moved up and down like arms as the whales swam. The tall fin that stood straight up on each of the whale's backs was not as sharply pointed as a shark's, and their heads were shiny and bulged like the great black pot the bilge boys used for cooking. They were not terribly large, as Abigail had heard whales to be. Cailin was only about twice as long as Abigail was tall, and Angel was probably three times Abigail's height. Ryan, the biggest whale, was far more massive than Angel.

The most amazing thing about the whales, Abigail 38 noticed, was that their mouths seemed to be curved in a genuine smile. Once Angel passed by with Cailin and playfully opened her mouth as if she would bite her calf, and Abigail saw that the mother whale had a mouthful of widely separated peglike teeth. She only nudged Cailin, though, not hurting her, and the baby rolled onto her back and mewed in pleasure as if the game were a lot of fun.

The entire pod seemed to play in the moonlight. Farther away, probably one hundred yards from the ship, Ryan flung himself entirely out of the water, completed a half turn in midair, and fell back onto his side with a tremendous splash. The whale's landing created a huge wave and a great swirl of foam, and Abigail was certain that everyone on both ships must have heard the commotion. *Why can't he be* quiet? *He'll have to be silent if he doesn't want to get into trouble.*

She cast a quick glance over her shoulder and noticed with dismay that the dark sky had begun to lighten in the east. Overhead, a seaman's strong voice called: "Oceans alive, look off the port bow! Show a leg, there, look alive! We're going to get a whale today!"

Horrified, Abigail heard the muffled thunder of the sailors overhead and knew that soon the shallop would fly toward the *Orca Blue* to begin the day's bloody work.

Go now, her heart cried as she leaned over the windowsill and gazed at her beloved whales. *Do not tarry! The time for playing has passed!*

She heard the shallop splash into the water; the seamen had wasted no time dallying over their morning chores. *Go! Go away!* she thought, wishing she had the courage to open her mouth and warn them to flee.

But the splash of the boat had apparently alerted Ryan. He lifted his head from the water and snapped his jaws together in a loud warning that sounded like a huge trunk closing. Instantly the other whales dove, and within a moment the shimmering sea was silent once again.

39

* * *

The splash of the shallop woke Kimberly, and her first thought was relief that she wouldn't have to endure the frustration of trying to teach the younger ones on this day. With the men of the *Seven Brothers* involved in a whale hunt, she was certain that no one would be able to think about alphabets and numbers.

The babble of voices rose outside the ship's windows, and she sat up and raised her head to look out and over at the *Orca Blue*. A dozen men from the *Seven Brothers* were already climbing up a rope ladder to the whaling ship's deck, and Captain Moab was standing by the ship's rail, his face glowing with expectation and delight. Thatcher, Christian, Brooke, Ethan, and the twins were lined like toy soldiers along the windows, with younger children peering out in the gaps between the older ones.

The companionway stairs creaked behind her, and Kimberly turned in time to see Squeege descend into the children's hold. "Are you not fishing today?" she called to him, a teasing note in her voice. "Or can Captain Blade not spare you?"

"I have no liking for whaling," Squeege said, his dark face flushing. He paused and thrust his hands into the waistband of his breeches. "And the captain says I'm too valuable to be lost in such a foolish attempt. Whaling is a desperate and dangerous venture, and we've kept our best hands aboard. The captain was willing to risk a lot to get the provisions we need, but he'd be a fool to risk his most useful men. A ship won't sail herself, you know."

"I'm glad you didn't go," Kimberly said, standing. She walked toward the window and peered through a space between Thatcher's and Ethan's shoulders. "Will we be able to watch the hunt from here?"

"Aye, 'tis likely," Squeege said, coming to stand behind her. The crowd at the window automatically shifted to make room for the bosun's ponderous form, for the children knew he would explain everything to them as they watched. "Those skiffs on the whaler's deck," he said, pointing to six long, narrow boats lined up in an orderly row upon the upper deck of the *Orca Blue*. "Those are whaleboats, designed solely for the harvesting of whales."

"They look like any other boats to me," Thatcher said, squinting through the bright rays of the rising sun as he studied the other ship.

"Ah, but they're not," Squeege answered. "You'd see the difference right off if you were sitting in one. There's

40

a slot at the bow through which the harpoon line runs.
Just behind it is a thwart with a clumsycleat to support
the harpooner's knee when he stabs the harpoon into the
whale."

"Ugh," Kimberly said, shuddering, "it all sounds
awful."

"How do they manage it?" Wingate asked. "How
can you get close enough to stab a whale?"

"Whales have a blind spot above their heads,"
Squeege said, shrugging. "A whale can see to his right
and left, but he can't see what's above him. The whalers
row until they spot the whales, then they wait above for
one of the creatures to come up for air. It may be two or
three minutes, but when he does, the whalers will fling
the harpoon like a javelin."

"They're so big," Ethan said, his brown eyes wide
with horror at the mention of such violence. "Surely one
harpoon can't kill them."

"You're right," Squeege said, leaning against the
wall. "When the animal is harpooned, he will dive and
swim as fast as he can. The harpoon is tied to a line,
though, and it will spin out more quickly than the eye can
see. The whaleboats have a bucket of water near the bow
for the men to cool the line as it runs out. I've seen two
hundred feet of rope disappear like magic over the edge,
then it will angle away from the boat and pull the whalers
through the water faster than any wind ye can imagine."

"They're setting out," Brooke called, and Kimberly
and the others turned their attention from Squeege back
to the *Orca Blue*. All six whaleboats had been lowered into
the water and were manned with six men in each. Four
men in the center sat at the oars, and one man sat in the
back to steer. The sixth man, who stood at the front, held
a slender harpoon in his hand as he scanned the waters
with narrowed eyes.

From where she sat, Kimberly could see that kegs of

41

fresh water and provisions were being handed down to the men in the boats. "How long do they expect to stay out?" she asked, alarmed. "Surely we won't be anchored here more than a few hours—"

"'Tis unlikely," Squeege said, his homely face rearranging itself into a grin. "But a man can get awful hot and thirsty while waiting for a whale to spend its energy and surrender."

Kimberly chewed on her thumbnail and turned back to the window. The front man's harpoon was tied to a long line that ended in a tub, and the rear man at each boat carried a hatchet to cut the line in an emergency. A stout post rose from the stern of the whaleboat, and Kimberly didn't want to ask why a post was necessary. She had a feeling the post was for tying up the dead whale as it was carried to the big ship.

"Thar she blows!" one of the men shouted, and every eye turned in the direction where his bony finger pointed. A spout of mist rose at a distance in the west, and Kimberly could see that the water moved differently in that area.

Behind her, she heard a choking sound, and when she turned she saw Abigail standing behind the others, her face deathly pale. "What's wrong, Abigail?" Kimberly whispered, but her question was drowned in the noise and excitement as the whaleboats got underway.

Turning again to the window, Kimberly saw the men raise their oars and start into furious motion, churning the sea. Caught up in the exhilaration of the chase, the children cheered.

The whaleboats were out of sight in ten minutes, and Captain Blade gave the order to raise the sails and follow at a leisurely pace. Squeege left the children so he could attend to his duties, and Kimberly forgot about Abigail's frightened face and hugged the windowsill, not willing to miss a moment of the whaling adventure.

6

Swim, whales, swim! The refrain repeated itself over and over in Abigail's head. She bit her lip until it bled, afraid to look out the window. Standing behind the others, she could hear the excited calls of the seamen, the steady lap of the waves against the departing whaleboats, the excitement in the children's voices as they cheered the whalers on.

"Quiet!" Captain Moab barked from the deck of his ship, and Abigail automatically cringed as the other children dropped their voices to a low murmur.

"I heard some of the men say that whales have keen hearing," Thatcher explained in a hoarse whisper. "If they hear a strange noise, they'll dive and be lost to the whalers."

Please, someone be noisy! Abigail stamped her feet in frustration, but her friends paid her no attention as they gazed out at the sea. Gathering her courage, she shouldered her way through the crowd at the window and flashed her eyes across the waters. The *Seven Brothers* had raised her sails and followed a steady distance from the whaleboats, and Abigail could see the whales swimming ahead. Leisurely rolling and blowing as they made their way across the water, they were apparently unaware of the danger that shadowed them. Ryan flung himself out of the water in an exuberant leap, and the harpooners pointed their boats toward him and the oarsmen doubled their efforts. The steady *clomp, clomp* of the oars rubbing against the oarlocks was the only sound now. Everyone in the whaleboats and aboard the ships waited for the outcome of the chase.

The whaleboats drew closer to their prey. Without a sound, the harpooner in the first boat rose to his feet and positioned himself with one foot in the bottom of the boat, the knee of his other leg braced against the notched board in the boat's bow. Ryan rose again, snorting through his blowhole, then sank beneath the water. The whaleboat lay directly behind him, securely in his blind spot.

The harpooner raised his weapon, balanced it in his hand, and seemed to calculate the area of water where Ryan would next rise. He bobbed his head as if he were counting to himself, then let the harpoon fly just as Ryan surfaced again for a breath of life-giving air.

The harpoon struck deep, and Abigail's eyes narrowed in pain as Ryan abruptly dove. The line attached to the harpoon whipped out of the tub in a steady hum, and the men in the whaleboat stayed well clear of its flying length. Abigail felt her heart leap into her throat as Ryan swam for his life, and her eyes filled with tears as she imagined the pain and shock the whale must be feeling. *I'm so sorry,* her inner voice cried. *I tried to warn you!*

Like a sled behind a charging horse, the whaleboat surged through the water, sending up sheets of spray along its sides and leaving a trail of shining wake. Ryan had the strength of twenty horses, and soon the whale-boat was lost to sight.

* * *

By the time the *Seven Brothers* and the *Orca Blue* caught up to the whalers, Kimberly could see that the whale had tired. The whaleboat that had harpooned him waited quietly near the animal's black head. The harpoon line hung slack in the water, and a second boat was moving toward the wounded animal.

"He gave us a merry chase!" one of the men called up to Captain Blade. "He broke from the water more than once, and the other whales followed until our mates managed to drive them away. The pod has scattered now, and the other boats are out hoping for an easy catch."

Kimberly was amazed when a keening wail filled the air and even the ship's timbers vibrated with the sorrowful cry. Part whimper, part roar, the dreadful protest was the saddest sound Kimberly had ever heard. The whale seemed to know that he was dying.

"Caa'ing whale," she heard Captain Blade remark. "The Scots gave them that name because they make that terrible sound when they're dying."

The exhausted whale floated on the surface, and Kimberly could hear its labored breathing through its blowhole. Rowing quietly and slowly, the second whale-boat came up behind the animal. Holding a long, slender lance, the front man stood ready and waited until the bow of the boat bumped the whale's side. At that instant, he leaned forward and threw his weight on the lance, driving it into the whale's body with enough force to push the blade into the whale's lungs. As soon as the oarsmen heard the man's triumphant cry, they began desperately pulling as hard as they could to propel the boat away from the whale.

The reason for their concentration was immediately

45

obvious. As the mighty whale received the lance, it reared out of the water, its massive tail whipping into the air. When the tremendous tail slammed back into the water, a colossal sheet of spray covered the area, and for a moment Kimberly thought rain had begun to fall.

During the tumult, another whale suddenly rose up from beyond the circle of spray and charged toward the whaleboats. With a roar, the defending whale leapt through the water like a greyhound, then attempted to butt the rope from the wounded whale. One of the harpooners took aim at the attacking creature and tossed his harpoon like a spear, but his aim was misguided, and the pointed lance merely glanced off the tough, black hide and fell into the churning waters.

But the blow was enough to warn the defender away. When the air finally cleared, the two whaleboats were well out of the way, their occupants dripping with seawater. The whalers wore the triumphant looks of men who had faced deadly risks and won, and the great beast floated belly-up in the water.

The harpooner in the whaleboat that had roped the animal passed the line to the sailor sitting at the stern. This man looped the rope around the stout pole at the back of the narrow boat. While Captain Moab and his men whistled and cheered, the whalers rowed the huge mammal toward the *Orca Blue*.

Kimberly watched in silence as the men approached. Four of the other whaleboats, each empty-handed, appeared on the horizon and rowed rapidly to lend a hand with the prize catch. The worried whale disappeared, and though the men who lined the decks of the *Orca Blue* and the *Seven Brothers* smiled broadly at the sight of their trophy, Kimberly felt a keen sense of loss. Behind her, Abigail sniffed, and Kimberly turned in time to see the red-haired girl wipe her eyes and nose on her sleeve. Her face was red and blotchy from crying, and

46

Kimberly was surprised that she had felt the animal's loss so keenly. But, she remembered, Abigail had seen whales in the water before and liked them well enough to embroider a picture of them.

She was about to say something to comfort Abigail, but one of the seamen shouted, and Kimberly turned back to the window. From out of the deep blue water, the second whale had reappeared and surfaced from an angle that allowed her to take the tail of the dead whale in her mouth. Wrestling the body away from the whaleboat, she gently closed her mouth around her wounded companion and swam away, once again unwinding the whalers' coiled rope.

"Pull him in!" Captain Moab shouted as the whaleboat spun and the men scrambled to their positions. "She'll take him from ye if ye don't wind him in!"

"What's that whale doing?" Kimberly whispered, her hands gripping the windowsill. "Doesn't it know that the other one is dead?"

"I think she's trying to keep it alive," Ethan answered, his dark eyes clouding with concern. "See how she dives for a moment and then surfaces with the body in her mouth? She's trying to bring him to the surface so he can breathe."

"How sad." The words clotted in her throat. "Do you suppose—"

"They have feelings for one another?" Wingate finished, gazing somberly at the scene. "Who can say? We are not whales; we cannot speak their language or know what they think."

"Or if they think at all," Ethan added.

"They do," Kimberly said, still watching the pathetic sight of the whale trying to revive the dead animal. "I'm certain they do. I didn't know until I heard the whale crying, but I know it now."

A second whaleboat rowed out to the first and

47

helped the men pull on the line, and within the space of half an hour the surviving whale gave up and swam slowly out to sea. Once again, the seamen brought the dead whale to the side of the *Orca Blue* and lashed it tight. Kimberly watched with morbid fascination as the whalers began the work of "cutting in." The *Orca Blue's* officers, wearing metal spikes strapped to the heels of their boots to keep them from slipping, climbed onto the whale's carcass. With long-handled spades they cut away long strips of skin with blubber attached. Kimberly crinkled her nose as the whalers cut a hole into the end of each strip and slipped a hook through the hole. The seamen on the *Orca Blue's* deck tugged on the ropes, pulling the strips of skin and blubber off the whale's body and onto the deck of the ship.

As the *Orca Blue's* crew bloodied the waters with their work, the sharp, pointed fins of sharks began to appear in the water. The men of the *Seven Brothers* climbed into their shallop and rowed hastily back to their own vessel. Kimberly shivered when she realized how close the whalers came to death each time one of them stepped from the safety of the ship onto the whale's carcass. One wrong step and a man would be in the water, surrounded by hungry sharks.

48

Soon the big body had been completely stripped. The whalers climbed onto the rigging at the side of the ship, unlashed the dead body, and allowed it to float away as food for the encircling sharks.

The skin and blubber on the deck was immediately cut into huge chunks and tossed into the large pots that hung over fires burning on brick beds. Once heated, the blubber cooked down into oil, which the whalers ladled out into copper tanks. As the sun sank slowly into the western sky, light from the two blazing fires upon the deck of the whaling ship lit the children's hold.

"Why do they have to kill the whales?" Kimberly

whispered to Ethan as they sat together in the darkness and watched the whalers at work. "They don't eat the whale meat, do they?"

Ethan shook his head. "'Tis for the oil. Whale oil gives a bright light and has no bitter smell. 'Tis used to make soap, paint, and perfume."

Heavy, booted steps sounded on the deck overhead, and Kimberly knew that Captain Blade and Squeege were also watching the men of the *Orca Blue*. "One more day, and we'll have our provisions," Captain Blade said, his voice as quiet as the night shadows. "I'll be glad to be away from the whalers. I have no love for this kind of work. When that whale attempted to rescue the other—well, I can't think of them as dumb beasts. That whale fought as bravely as any man I've ever seen."

"There will be more fighting on the morrow," Squeege answered. "I heard the men of the *Orca Blue* say that they plan to kill a calf early in the day. 'Twill bait one of the larger whales, mayhap its mother."

Captain Blade sighed. "We'd better sleep, then. Tomorrow will be a long day."

* * *

Abigail stiffened as she heard the conversation between the captain and Squeege. She had died a thousand deaths and felt her heart break in a million places as Ryan died and Angel tried to save him. Would they really try to kill Cailin and Angel, too? It had been a terrible day, nearly unbearable. After Ryan's death, Abigail did not venture again near the windows. She remained in the shadows of the hold instead, wanting to ignore the carnage but unable to, for the other children's cries revealed everything that happened on the sea.

And tomorrow the whalers would row out and search for a calf and its mother! She had to do something,

49

to warn someone. But who? And how could she make them understand?

Frantically, Abigail stood up in the hold and peered through the darkness. Nearly all the others were asleep; only Kimberly, Wingate, and Ethan sat at the window, still watching the whalers at work. Gathering her resolve, Abigail walked to them and tapped Kimberly firmly on the shoulder.

"What, Abigail?" Kimberly asked, turning around. "Can't you sleep?"

Abigail shook her head and pointed toward the whalers' ship.

"I know. We're watching them, too," Kimberly answered, turning her face toward the window again. "'Tis gruesome, but Ethan says whale oil is important."

Abigail shook her head and sighed in frustration. They wouldn't understand. How could they? They hadn't heard the whale song. They hadn't seen the mother and her playful baby.

Abigail looked around for something to write with, but there was no paper or pen, and she couldn't find Kimberly's lump of charcoal in the darkness.

50

There was nothing to do but approach the captain himself. The captives weren't supposed to climb to the upper deck without the captain's express permission, but some things were worth the risk. And he had sounded sympathetic when he spoke with Squeege.

Abigail took a deep breath, lifted her chin, and began to climb the companionway stairs.

* * *

"What are you doin' aft, missy?" Squeege's rough voice caught Abigail by surprise, and she jerked in alarm.

Squeege's eyes softened at the frightened look on her face, but his voice remained stern. "You should be below, and you ought to be asleep by now. What's the trouble? Are you sick?"

Abigail shook her head, then pointed toward the small door that led to the captain's cabin.

"Captain Blade's asleep by now, of certain, and he'll have both our hides if we wake him. Why don't you see him on the morrow?"

Abigail shook her head frantically, then spread her palm and used her other hand to imitate writing. She had never really gone to school, but one of the scullery maids from Mistress Ludlow's house had taught her how to write the alphabet and a few words. If she was very careful and concentrated very hard, maybe she could make the captain understand that the men must not kill the baby whale and its mother.

Squeege must have read the desperation in her eyes, for after pausing a moment, he thrust his hands into the waistband of his breeches and jerked his chin toward the captain's cabin. "I'll see if he's still awake," he said, looking grim. "If he is, you will have a chance to tell him what's got you so bothered. If not, girl, you will just have to wait till the morrow."

Abigail sighed and nodded her agreement, then followed Squeege to the captain's cabin.

* * *

DO NOT LET THEM KIL THE BABY WALE. IT IS MY FRIND.

Abigail thrust her note toward the captain, who read it without changing the stony expression on his face. "How can a whale be your friend?" he asked, sliding the parchment across the table toward her. "And how do you know there's even a baby whale out there?"

Abigail picked up the feather quill and dipped it into the ink again. Slowly, carefully, she penned another message: WE MUST NOT KIL MORE WALES.

Captain Blade took the note, scanned it, then crumpled it in his hand. "Bah, girl, there are thousands of whales in the sea. Millions of them, don't you see? For this you bother me? We need provisions, child, or we will not make it to Virginia. Would you rather help Captain Moab or starve on the ocean?"

Abigail's eyes filled with tears before the anger in his face. She shook her head in confusion.

The captain's brows knitted in a frown. "I'll admit 'tis no great pleasure to hunt such gentle creatures. But whales are not people, child. They are animals and were put here for man's use. They're fish. They can't be your friends, and you're wrong to think of them as anything more than creatures of the sea. So go below like a good girl, and don't bother me again with this nonsense—especially not in the dark of night!"

Abigail bit her lip as she fought back the emotion that threatened to erupt in a fit of angry tears. Glancing off to her right as she left the captain's cabin, she saw the fires still burning on the *Orca Blue's* deck. Between the ships, the water glinted red with the blood of the massacred whale.

Saturday, May 29

7

Abigail awoke to a gray and grim Saturday morning. The mood in the hold was strangely subdued, and the children who moved about at all did so with quiet, muffled steps, as if they half expected someone to order them back to sleep. Maybe the strange mood was due to the overcast weather, or maybe the minor melodies of Ethan's Sabbath songs had cast a pall over the company. But whether or not the others would admit it, Abigail thought the infinitely sorrowful spirit in the air was a remnant of yesterday's slaughter of the whale. Though London had been anything but a gentle city, Abigail had never seen anything as vicious as the hunt and killing she had witnessed the day before.

In a rush of bitter remembrance, she recalled that the men of the *Seven Brothers* were to work again with the whalers of the *Orca Blue*. And today, Captain Moab had said, they would attempt to spear a calf in order to trap a large mother whale.

A headache began to pound behind Abigail's forehead, and she leaned her head down into her hands, wishing the world away. She did not want to sew, to look out the window, or to listen to the others tell their stories and argue about what they'd become in Virginia. A crown of gloom settled about her head, and she closed her eyes and wished, just for a moment, that she had never heard the whales' song. If she had never learned to love them, she would not be feeling this heartbreaking pain.

This terrible burden weighed her down until she felt she would drown in her own sorrow. If only she could tell someone what she was feeling! But no one on the ship could read her mind, so her secret would remain locked away, hidden forever behind the mask of hopelessness she wore on her face.

* * *

Kimberly sighed in satisfaction when she woke and caught a glimpse of the gray sky. The air was very still and dark, heavy with impending rain. The youngsters would be more subdued today, and perhaps she could have class without having to yell at them. She sat up and ran her fingers through her long brown hair to comb it, then pulled it into a knot at the nape of her neck. Joshua, the eight-year-old sprite who had given her so much trouble the last time she tried to teach, sprinted by on his way to the window. "The men are loading the shallop to join the whalers," he said, carelessly stepping on her foot as he ran past. "C'mon, let's get a look at them as they go!"

"Oh, nay, you'll not get near that window," Kimberly cried, anger propelling her forward. She reached out and grabbed the collar of Joshua's shirt. "We're having class today, and I'll not brook any arguing. And you owe me an apology, young man, for you stepped on my foot just now!"

54

"I did?" Joshua said, his face like that of a surprised angel.

But Kimberly knew better. He was a mischievous brat, and she'd tried to deal with him gently and failed. Quiet warnings and firm rebukes accomplished nothing with Joshua, nor with most of the others. It was only when she stamped her foot and yelled that they settled down to listen. So if she had to do it again today . . .

She screwed her face into the meanest glare she could imagine and stared at the circle of eager youngsters who'd been about to follow Joshua to the window. They shrank back, visibly upset by her scowl, and she raised a hand and pointed toward the mainmast. "You will all sit down there!" she commanded, stamping her foot upon the heavy wooden planking for emphasis. "You will not move, not one of you, until you can each spell *cat* and *rat* and *hat*. Do you understand?"

The children cowered before her raised voice, but they nodded and retreated as a group to the empty space by the mainmast. Kimberly watched with satisfaction, then glanced over at her friends. Wingate and Thatcher were watching with puzzlement in their eyes, Brooke's mouth was open in surprise, and Abigail leaned against the wall with tears streaming down her face.

The sight of Abigail's tears sent a twinge of guilt through Kimberly's heart, but she quickly shrugged it off. How dare Abigail feel sorry for those noisy brats! She'd yell, too, if she had a voice to yell with and the job of managing the rowdy youngsters.

Kimberly stalked over to stand in front of Abigail. "You're not making my job any easier," Kimberly said, crossing her arms as she glared down at the silent girl. "I'm only doing what I have to do, and here you sit all weepy and sad, feeling sorry for the brats. Well, get over your tears, Abigail. I don't care what you think."

A hurt expression filled Abigail's eyes, and fresh tears began to flow.

"Hey," Wingate said, raising his hand in Abigail's defense. He wore a horrified expression of disapproval. "What the devil has come over you, Kimberly?"

"Nothing," Kimberly snapped, moving toward her students. "Nothing at all. Now, don't you all have jobs to do? 'Tis not a holiday, you know. Let's get to work."

She could feel their eyes boring into her back as she sat down with the young ones, but Kimberly hardened her resolve to be firm and began her lesson. "Cat: *c-a-t*. Who can spell *rat?*"

* * *

The air of late afternoon seemed lifeless, the fading light melancholy and filled with shadows as Kimberly tucked her kirtle around her ankles and rested her chin on her raised knees. She'd been firm and terse all day, keeping total and absolute control over her young charges, and now she felt absolutely limp with weariness. Everyone onboard the ship seemed to be in a foul mood. Abigail had sniffed and sniveled all day, never once allowing Kimberly to catch her eye and offer a smile as an apology. Wingate had ignored Kimberly at lunch, and Thatcher had gone out of his way to make sure she heard him tell Brooke, "Kimberly's become a witch in the last two days. What do you suppose is wrong with her?"

She wanted to tell them there was nothing wrong with her, that she had to be tough if she was going to accomplish what she had set out to do. Her mother had believed that God put them aboard the *Seven Brothers* to help the children through the ocean crossing and prepare them for life in America. Kimberly was only trying to fulfill her mother's plans. She had tried being nice to everyone, but the young ones just ignored her and kept on with their talking and playing and running around the ship. She'd tried being firm, but they laughed at her as if she were only pretending to be grown-up, something she wasn't—yet. They only obeyed when she screamed and yelled, so if she had to yell and scream, she'd do it. She was only trying to do what her mother wanted to do.

But your mother wouldn't become angry and raise her voice, an inner voice reminded her. *She would just speak to the others, and they would listen. Right now, if your mother were here, she'd be surrounded by little ones begging for a story. But where are the children who usually cling to your kirtle, Kimberly? They're afraid you'll yell at them, so they're sitting with Brooke instead. But Brooke can't tell the stories you can tell. Brooke doesn't know the Bible the way you do. She can't teach them the things your mother wanted you to.*

"What can I do?" she whispered in a broken voice. Troubled and lonely, she lay down upon the hard wooden flooring alone until sleep finally claimed her.

* * *

Abigail couldn't sleep. Ever since the men of the *Seven Brothers* had returned empty-handed in the shallop, she had been staring at the dark surface of the sea in a state of hopefulness. The whalers hadn't caught a whale today! The pod must have escaped to waters far away. But because Captain Blade had kept his word, at sunset Captain Moab and the *Orca Blue* sent over forty-eight casks of provisions. Soon after the kegs had been stored in the lower hold, Captain Blade gave the order to make sail, and the captives' ship began to slowly pull away from the whaler.

Now the *Orca Blue* was only a black silhouette against the violet sky, and the orange-red splashes of her fires were swallowed by the night. She would undoubtedly continue to hunt and kill the whales, so Abigail did something she never thought she would do—she lifted

57

her heart in prayer and asked God to guide the whales to safety. There was no one else to help them.

She felt an odd and unexplainable peace when she had finished praying. The wind picked up, and Abigail felt the ship climb the creaming slope of a wave, then slip down its roaring top and travel smoothly down into the hollow. Captain Blade gave hurried orders above to hoist the storm staysails, and men pounded the decks as they hurried to obey.

But all else was silent. Beneath the ship, no whales sang. And Abigail was glad, for the silence meant Angel and Cailin were safe and far away.

Sunday, May 30

8

Kimberly fastened a stern eye upon the younger children as they sat in neatly lined rows in the hold. On the deck above, Captain Blade was reading the Sunday service from the *Book of Common Prayer*, and Kimberly thought it just as important for the children to hear the word of God as to learn to spell.

"Oh, that men would therefore praise the Lord for his goodness and declare the wonders that he doeth for the children of men," the captain read. His voice echoed throughout the ship, and even though the children couldn't see him through the open hatchway, still they felt the conviction in his words and the solemn earnestness in his voice. "Then they would offer unto him the sacrifice of thanksgiving, and tell out his works with gladness! They that go down to the sea in ships, and occupy their business in great waters, these men see the works of the Lord, and his wonders in the deep. He hath created great whales, and every living creature that moveth, which the waters bring forth abundantly. And at his word the stormy wind ariseth, which lifteth up the waves thereof. They are carried up to the heaven, and down again to the deep; their soul melteth away because of the trouble. They reel to and fro, and stagger like a drunken man, and are at their wit's end."

The sound of giggling distracted Kimberly, and she turned and saw Joshua cross his eyes and sway back and forth like a drunk. Impulsively, she reached out and slapped his foot. Every eye in the hold turned at the sharp sound, and she glared at Joshua, then lifted her gaze to meet the others' accusing eyes.

"He shouldn't be playing while the Scripture is being read," she whispered. No one answered, and Kimberly gave Joshua another stern look, then turned to face the companionway to hear the end of Captain Blade's reading.

"So when they cry unto the Lord in their trouble, he delivereth them out of their distress. For he maketh the storm to cease, so that the waves thereof are still. Then are they glad, because they are at rest: and so he bringeth them unto the haven where they would be."

60   As the captain continued with his reading and prayers, Kimberly allowed her mind to wander. The Lord had created whales even before he created the land animals and man himself, so the men of the *Orca Blue* had caught and killed one of God's oldest creations. And the whales were so powerful! With one flick of his tail the whale they caught could have destroyed a whaleboat, and had he chosen to ram the massive *Orca Blue*, he could have done serious damage. He had so much strength, but still God had given the whalers mastery over the animal. With a rope and rods of iron, they had subdued one of the mightiest and strongest animals on earth.

I used to be strong, Kimberly thought, remembering

her first days aboard the ship. *When Mama died, when Thatcher had his trouble with the pirates, when Brooke needed a friend—I was able to cope with everything. But now I'm tired, worn out by the little things like noise and a handful of squirmy, mischievous children.*

She imagined herself floating in the water like a whale while Joshua and the other children rode in a miniature boat and tossed nets at her head and pricked her with Abigail's sewing needles. One little prick, one thin rope wasn't much to fuss about, but when she was tired and the devilish little whalers just wouldn't go away, it was awfully hard to bear.

"Kimberly?" Wingate's voice broke through the fog of her daydream.

"What?" she said, smoothing her face so Wingate wouldn't guess what she'd been thinking.

"I want to talk to you," he said, jerking his head toward the back of the ship. "I know there's no such thing as privacy here, but if you'd rather only a few of the others heard our conversation, won't you come with me to the stern?"

Kimberly sighed and shook her head. "I know what you're going to say, Wingate. You're going to tell me that I'm being mean and harsh and that you and the others think I should stop. Right?"

Wingate's face clouded for a moment, then he nodded. "I wouldn't have been that blunt," he said, shrugging. "But yes, that's what I wanted to tell you. And I'm telling you this because I'm your friend."

"Well, if you're truly my friend, Wingate, you'll understand that I'm only doing what I have to do. So unless you're willing to give up the peace and quiet of mending canvas so you can teach the brats yourself, I suggest you leave me alone and let me tend to my work."

She gave him a stiff smile and raised her voice so that all the others could hear. "And if Brooke, or

61

Thatcher, or Ethan, or Christian, or even Abigail wants to take my place as teacher, then I'll willingly step aside and let someone else do the job. Otherwise, I'll thank you all to mind your own business and leave me be."

Wingate gaped at her in astonishment, and Kimberly stood and moved away with her chin held high.

* * *

After the Sunday service, the children took advantage of the captain's proclaimed day of rest to relax in the hold. A few napped, some daydreamed, others talked quietly in small groups. But everyone honored the quiet reverence of the afternoon, and no one dared disturb the peace.

Abigail sat by the window, her eyes scanning the wavelets that flecked the surface of the sea, her ears tuned to catch the low, moving sound of the whales' song. Still she heard nothing, and she was torn between feeling relieved and sad. She knew she ought to be glad that the whales were far away, but what if their paths crossed that of the *Orca Blue?* The *Seven Brothers* was once again underway for Virginia, and she would never see the whales again unless they chanced to follow the ship.

She pushed her bottom lip forward in thought. If only she could swim in the sea! Maybe she could find Angel and Cailin, call out a warning, and somehow direct them to waters where whalers did not hunt. If only she could speak their language and be *closer* to them.

On a sudden impulse, Abigail leapt up from her place and climbed down the companion ladder to the third hold. The three bilge boys who lived below blinked in surprise when they saw her, but she gave them a timid smile and moved without hesitation to the small trapdoor that led to the orlop deck, the lowest hold in the ship. A small leather strap had been nailed to the wooden planking of the hatch, and she placed her hand around the strap.

"I don't know what you're planning to do, but I wouldn't be raising that door if I were you," one of the bilge boys offered. "'Tis a powerful stench down there, and more rats than you can imagine, I'm sure. Please, miss, come away from there."

Abigail pretended she hadn't heard his warning and gave the strap a mighty tug. The swollen wood stuck for an instant, then groaned and broke free of the small square opening.

Peering into the darkness below, Abigail could see only black water that moved and shimmered in the dim light from above. This hold was below the water level, so there were no windows or openings for drainage or air. Rocks and old bricks lined the bottom of the orlop deck to provide the ship with stabilizing ballast, and whatever water was used on the upper decks for cooking, cleaning, or sanitation gradually filtered through to the orlop deck.

The stench assaulted her nostrils with the force of a physical blow. The deck reeked of squalor and rot and filth, but Abigail knew she would have to bear it if her plan were to work. Gingerly, she sat on the floor and lowered her feet through the opening.

"Miss," another of the boys called, coming toward her with a concerned expression on his face. "Whatever are you thinking? You can't be going below there."

Abigail didn't wait for him to stop her. She pushed off and allowed herself to fall into the darkness of the orlop. Her feet hit a layer of uneven rock, and she lost her balance and fell, hands first, into the water. Her stomach churned at the thought of what might be living in this murky pool, but Abigail blocked such thoughts from her mind and stood up, struggling to find her balance.

"Miss?" the faces of all three bilge boys appeared in the square opening above her head. "Miss, we're not coming down for you, do you understand? Now you come up here now, for your own sake. Come on into the light where we can see you."

Abigail squinted as she looked up at them, then waved them away and purposely stepped out of the square of light and into total darkness. Let them wonder about her. She'd be fine as long as she didn't allow herself to be afraid, and she'd know when she had accomplished her task.

Ignoring the boys' warning cries, she pressed forward into the living night.

* * *

After a quarter of an hour, the boys moved away from the opening, probably tired of calling her. Abigail closed her eyes—they weren't of much use in the darkness, anyway—and moved steadily through water that came up to her knees and felt slimy against her skin. Her kirtle, drawing up the water like a sponge, was completely soaked all the way to the waistband, but Abigail did not pause in her purpose. She walked until she felt the smooth wood of the ship's hull beneath her palms, then took a seat on a rock jutting out of the water.

She had wanted to get as close as possible to the whales, and here in the orlop deck she was underwater. Was it possible that sounds made from this dark place could travel through the sea? If she was capable of making a sound—and that was a big *if*—would the whales be able to hear her? Thatcher had said that whales had keen hearing. . . .

Her plan might work. And here in this splendid privacy, she could do what she had never dared to do before any other person—*make a sound.*

Fear of the unknown and untried knotted and writhed in her stomach. How, exactly, did people talk? How did they scream? sing? They opened their mouths and sound came out. But how?

As a child, Abigail had been told to remain silent. Later, as she had grown, she had always been too terrified of what people would think to attempt speaking. But now she must speak, or at least make a noise if the whales were to hear her. Their lives might even depend upon her success.

A confusing rush of anticipation and dread whirled inside her. She opened her mouth, took a deep breath, and thought of the whales' song.

"Aaaauuuuuuuuuooooooo," she cried, the sound flat and ugly to her ears. She clapped her hand over her mouth and closed her eyes so tightly that tears squeezed out from the corners.

No one laughed. No one screamed. It was possible that no one had even heard her.

Abigail trembled in every limb, and despite the cold of the water around her, sweat poured from her arms and face. "Aaauuuuuuoooooooooeeeeeeeeeee," she said, more quietly. Abigail found she could shift the sound by moving her lips. Closing her eyes, she concentrated on the memory of the sounds the whales made. By snapping her tongue against her teeth, she was able to imitate their clicking sounds.

Time sped by quickly, and Abigail was unaware of it, so hard she concentrated on her efforts. Her noises were nothing like the melodic voices of the whales and certainly bore no resemblance to normal speech, but she continued to practice until her head was light with exertion and her stomach rumbled from hunger.

Weary and discouraged, she pulled her dripping feet out of the water and propped her arms upon her knees. Pillowing her head upon her arms, she was about to fall asleep when she once again made the low sound of the whales' cry. An echo answered her, and she nodded drowsily in agreement, *Yes, it sounds just like that,* then her heart went into sudden shock. It was an actual whale's cry! Whether she had brought them or not, they had returned!

She splashed to the side of the ship and pressed her hands against the slimy walls, feeling for the vibrations of sound that had reached her. Another whale cry sounded, closer and stronger this time, and Abigail threw back her head and whooped for joy. The whales sang, and she sang. They cried, and Abigail answered until she was nearly too exhausted to climb out of the orlop deck.

Finally, though, tired and happy, she found the hand-holds in the wall and climbed up to the lower hold. The bilge boys lay sleeping on bags of grain, and Abigail walked past them and climbed to the children's hold above. With some surprise she noticed that full darkness had descended and most of the other children were asleep.

"Whew!" Brooke called as Abigail tiptoed past on her way to the window. "Abigail, what have you been into? You stink!"

Smiling, Abigail remembered the terrible stench of the whales' breath. She had talked to the whales; maybe she even smelled like them now.

The midnight moon shone through the sky as Abigail took her place by the window. As the *Seven Brothers* moved steadily through the water, the miles streaming behind her, the ship's white path was occasionally broken by the black shape of a whale dancing in the moonlight.

Monday, May 31

9

"Whale ho! Thar she blows!"

The lookout's cry woke Abigail, and she sat bolt upright. The whales couldn't have remained with them through the night—could they?

The other children milled about the windows as they pointed out to sea. "Look at all of them," Kimberly was saying, her eyes round with awe. "I've never seen so many."

"They're swimming so close," Thatcher remarked, leaning on the windowsill with his elbows. "If we weren't up so high, we could almost reach out and touch them."

Abigail sprang to her feet and pressed through the crowd until she could see the water. The waves were calm this morning, stirred only by the dark forms of the whales, who swam lazily about the ship. From here Abigail could clearly hear their whistles, clicks, and squeals. So could everyone else.

"What noises they make!" Brooke said, her pretty face wreathed in wonder. "I thought whales roared, but such teeny, tiny sounds come out of their mouths."

"Not their mouths," Ethan corrected her. "For they make the sounds while their mouths are still under water. The noises you hear are coming from their blowholes."

"Their what?" Brooke asked, crinkling her nose.

"Those small holes on the top of their heads," Ethan answered, pointing to a large whale as it surfaced directly in front of him. "'Tis what they use for breathing. They eat through their mouths, I suppose, and breathe through those round holes."

Just then the whale under observation blew a loud gust of air through his blowhole, spewing water from his back and raining down a shower of moisture upon the gathered children. "Ugh!" Brooke squealed, wiping droplets from her hands and face. "It stinks! What was that smell, his breath?"

"Seems likely," Kimberly said, resting her chin in her hands as she stared out to sea.

The seamen on the deck above seemed to be as fascinated as the children by the whale pod surrounding the ship, and Abigail could hear their comments. "Look at the great knob of flesh on that one's forehead," one of the sailors exclaimed. "If he chose to ram this ship, how long do ye think we'd remain afloat?"

"Mayhap a quarter hour, if God smiled on us," Squeege answered. "I once saw one of these caa'ing whales ram a killer whale in self-defense. That knob of flesh on their heads is nothing but a melon of thick fat. It can burst the internal organs of a shark or other enemy while it cushions the head of the caa'ing whale. They are gentle animals, to be certain, but they can hold their own in a fight."

"I wonder how many musket balls 'twould take to make one of 'em go belly-up," the other sailor said.

Abigail darted for the companionway as she heard the muffled rattle of a musket being cocked and lifted. She knew she'd probably get a scolding or be forced to miss a meal for venturing onto the deck without permission, but she couldn't let that man shoot the whales!

Her heavy shoes thundered on the deck as she ran toward the sailor, a tall, thin man who squinted down the barrel of his long musket. Without stopping to think, Abigail jumped onto his back, fastening herself to him like a leech. The man turned, his mouth opening in amazement, and the gun discharged and clattered to the deck, sending a cloud of black smoke into the air. Every man on ship ducked for cover.

"That's enough, missy!" Squeege shouted, pulling Abigail off the sailor.

"What devil has possessed her?" the sailor asked, rubbing his neck where Abigail's hands had gripped it.

Though her hands still trembled, Squeege released her, then looked around to see what damage the musket ball had done. One of the other seamen pointed toward the tall mainmast. There, exactly at the height of a man's head, the musket ball lay embedded in the heavy wood.

"Thank God the captain wasn't standing there," Squeege said, lowering his voice as he glanced around. His gaze shifted toward the bewildered sailor. "Put your musket away before someone is hurt."

The creak of the captain's cabin door silenced all further conversation, and the men on deck stiffened as Captain Blade came out onto the deck. He sniffed the air as his dark eyes fell upon the bullet in the mainmast, then he thrust his hands behind his back and stared at the frightened sailor who held the gun.

"We do not shoot at whales," Captain Blade finally said, every word clipped and carefully enunciated. "We do not fish for whales. We are a transport ship, a cargo ship, and we will not waste time dallying for sport. Do you understand, or must I tie you to yonder mainmast for a flogging to remind you?"

"I understand," the seaman replied, bobbing nervously before the captain. "It won't happen again, Captain. You have my word on it. I'll put the musket away and not take it out again."

"Do that." Captain Blade's dark eyes fell upon Abigail. "And you, missy, what are you doing out of your place? You know this deck is for the seamen."

Abigail nodded and moved slowly toward the narrow staircase leading to the children's hold. Kimberly and Thatcher stood on the stairs, peering out to see what had happened above, but they moved back down as Abigail descended. *Mayhap Captain Blade understands*, Abigail thought as she lifted her stiff kirtle so she could climb down. *He won't let the men hurt the whales, and he wasn't nearly as fierce as I thought he might be.*

Smiling, she joined the other children to watch the whales play.

* * *

Kimberly observed the scene between Abigail and Captain Blade with a great deal of interest. After Abigail had rejoined the others, Kimberly moved toward Thatcher and pulled him into a corner. "What's going on with Abigail?" she whispered, trying not to attract the others' attention.

"She smells terrible," Thatcher answered. "Like garbage that's been left out in the sun. I know none of us are a bouquet, but she smells absolutely the worst—"

"She disappeared yesterday for a long time," Kimberly went on. "Do you suppose she went down into the lower hold to do something with the bilge boys? Mayhap she's helping them cook or something."

"Nay," Thatcher answered. "They wouldn't do

anything without asking the captain first. They wouldn't want to risk a flogging."

"She's been very unhappy," Kimberly went on. "She cries for no reason."

"Welladay, do you think she's happy about being on a kidnapper's ship?"

"None of us are, but we shed our tears weeks ago. Abigail wasn't at all upset when we left London, so why should she cry now?"

"Mayhap she has fallen in love with one of the boys—"

Kimberly frowned. "Who?"

Thatcher shrugged. "Wingate? He helps her with the sails."

Kimberly shook her head. "She loves him not. If she did, she'd be trying to make herself pretty, not foul and evil-smelling. Unless of course," Kimberly gave him a teasing smile, "she thought herself in love with *you*."

"Bah." Thatcher made a face. "You're right. The girl is not in love. What else have you noticed?"

Kimberly chewed her thumbnail, thinking. "She stopped sewing the sails a few days ago," she said. "I found her embroidering a picture upon the canvas. 'Twas a very nice picture of two whales—smiling, they were. A large whale and a small one, like a mother and a baby."

"What is so unusual about that?"

Kimberly shrugged. "When has she had the opportunity to see whales? We've been at sea three weeks, and the whales we saw near the *Orca Blue* were the first I've seen. She sewed this picture before we met up with Captain Moab's ship."

Thatcher scratched the growth of straggly chin hair that promised to be a real beard some day. "Mayhap she knew the whales were near. Mayhap she has seen them before and couldn't tell us about them."

"But why is she so protective of them? She was up

71

those stairs awfully quick to stop that man with the musket."

Thatcher grinned. "Mayhap she talks to the whales. Of certain she doesn't talk to us."

Kimberly groaned and gave him a playful punch in the arm. "Will you stop being foolish? I'm trying to find a real answer, a way to understand her."

Thatcher's face grew serious. "What if she does talk to them? I've heard of stranger things. They say old man Creasely in London talked to his cat. There is nothing unusual in that, but the cat talked back until the day old man Creasely died."

"That's a silly old tale," Kimberly grumbled. "There's not a bit of truth in it. Nay, 'tis unthinkable and utterly impossible. Animals can't talk to people, and people of certain can't talk back."

"Can't they?" Thatcher answered, raising a brow. "I've heard that when a person loses one sense—his hearing, for example—the other senses grow keen. A deaf man will have good eyes, and a blind man good ears. Well, our Abigail has no voice, so who can say that God has not given her ears to understand the tongues of animals?"

72   Kimberly crinkled her nose. "Thatcher, you have been in the sun too long. Go away. I hear foolishness from the youngsters all day. I don't want to hear it from you too."

10

After threatening to make whale bait out of any child who talked or daydreamed during her lesson, Kimberly decided to teach what little she knew about whales. "The Bible tells a story about a man and a whale," she said, fixing her pupils with a stern eye. "God told Jonah to go preach to people in an evil city, but Jonah didn't want to go. He fled from God in a ship very much like this one, but God sent a storm that thrashed the boat upon the waves. The seamen were certain they would all perish in the sea, so Jonah told them to cast him overboard. 'Twas then that God sent the whale to swallow Jonah alive."

"I hesitate to correct you," Ethan said, standing. He regarded Kimberly with thoughtful brown eyes. "But the Hebrew word expressly says that God prepared a 'great fish.' My father has often pointed it out to me that nowhere does the prophet write that Jonah was swallowed by a whale."

Kimberly frowned. She wasn't thrilled that Ethan had dared to contradict her while she was trying to teach the younger ones, but his words brought a nagging doubt to her mind. What did the Bible say? Her mother had always said 'twas a whale that swallowed Jonah, and the idea made sense, since both whales and men breathe air.

"I know," Kimberly said, snapping her fingers. "Jesus himself said 'twas a whale that swallowed Jonah. In Matthew 'tis recorded that just as Jonah was three days and three nights in the whale's belly, so the Son of Man would be three days and three nights in the heart of the earth. But what does it matter if it was a whale or some other great fish? 'Twas a miracle, and Jesus' prediction came true."

"Jesus." Ethan frowned and took a step backward as if the name were distasteful to him. "We agree upon much, Kimberly, but we cannot agree upon the idea of Jesus. My father told me that Christians have hated the Jews for generations because they blame us for the man Jesus' death."

"He was more than a man, Ethan," Kimberly said, softening her voice. For an instant she forgot about her students and her lessons. It was more important to make sure Ethan understood the reason for her faith. "Jesus was a man, yet he was God. He was your Messiah, and he came to earth to be a sacrifice for sin that would allow us to enter a loving relationship with God."

"I fear God," Ethan said, folding his hands so tightly that Kimberly could see his knuckles whiten. "The Jew's purpose is to live a good life, to fill the mind with knowledge and the heart with acts of loving-kindness."

"Christians study and perform acts of kindness, too," Kimberly said, lifting her head so she could see clearly into Ethan's troubled eyes. "But we know that our small acts of goodness are nothing compared to God's holy purity. We can never measure up to his standards of perfection, so we trust Jesus to meet those standards for us. We place our trust in him, the Jewish Messiah, instead of in ourselves."

Ethan backed away from Kimberly's eager gaze. "I don't know much about this Jesus," he mumbled, leaving the circle of children at Kimberly's feet.

"We can talk later," Kimberly promised. As Ethan walked away, she turned back to her students, wiped the smile from her face, and sternly told them, "If Jesus said the great fish was a whale, then 'twas of certain a whale, and no doubt."

* * *

Abigail did not leave the window, but sat entranced as she watched the whales play. The calm waters that vexed Captain Blade and left the sails hanging in flaccid bulges from the yards seemed to delight her sea-dwelling friends. They rolled and dove and squealed noisily through their blowholes as if calling to the children who watched from the windows. Sometimes a large whale would charge through the water at great speed, leaving foaming swirls behind as he raced over the surface in a feat of athletic exuberance. Others sunned themselves just beneath the surface, relaxed and lazy in the water.

75

From where she watched, Abigail spent most of her time following Angel and Cailin with her eyes. Once she pushed her hands into the empty space outside the window, wishing she could touch them. As Wingate and the others clapped and enjoyed the whales, Abigail wished she had the voice to tell them about the night she had called to the whales and heard their reply. She wanted to tell the tragic story of Ryan's bravery. But she did not know how to make her sounds into words, and fear of ridicule kept her from trying.

It was enough to know that her human friends had met her whale friends and that all her friends were safe.

* * *

Kimberly dismissed her circle of students after a frustrating hour of teaching. None of the others had kept to their usual routines today—Wingate hadn't mended a single sail, Brooke had deserted Denni and Daryl for a seat at the window, and even Christian had neglected his duties as singer so he could sit next to Brooke and hear her describe everything the whales were doing. No one took his or her responsibilities seriously, and Kimberly felt her frustration churning into a slow, angry boil. She'd soon be yelling at all of them if they didn't get to work and stick to the routine they had agreed upon. If a pod of whales could make all of them forget about their work, what would a pack of dolphins do? A flock of seagulls? They were just looking for excuses not to work!

She leaned against the mizzenmast and crossed her arms. Deliberately keeping her eyes from the whales in the swirling waters outside, she fixed her eyes on the horizon. Somewhere beyond this patch of calm sea was a wind, for clouds scurried across the skyline and a ship's sails billowed full and free on the edge of the ocean—

She caught her breath. Another ship! The lookout must have lost his senses to the whales, for it was his job to cry out at any sign of another vessel, no matter how far away.

"Sail ho!" came the cry a minute later. Every eye in the children's hold lifted automatically, and a silence that was the holding of a hundred breaths fell upon the place. They did not know whether to expect pirates, friends, or foes.

"'Tis the *Orca Blue*," Brooke said, her voice heavy with relief. "At least we know they are friendly."

A muffled sob came from the window, and Kimberly glanced over to see Abigail crumpled there, her face as pale as paper and her eyes glowing green in the sunlight. "Is anything wrong?" Kimberly asked, hurrying to

Abigail's side. She lowered her voice. "You can tell me, Abigail. We've been so concerned about you. 'Tis obvious that you have not been yourself."

In answer, Abigail grabbed Kimberly's hand and stood up, pulling Kimberly to the companionway. Frantically, she pointed upward, then dropped Kimberly's hand and began to climb. "You want me to come with you," Kimberly said, following. "But why? Have you something to say to Squeege? To the captain?"

Abigail didn't attempt to answer, and by the time Kimberly had pulled herself out onto the upper deck, Abigail was already pounding on the door to Captain Blade's cabin. "What is this?" he roared, swinging the door open. He paused to glare at the girls, then looked past them to give Squeege an annoyed look. "Can't you keep the youngsters below? This is becoming a habit, Squeege, and I don't like it."

"I'll bar the hatch," Squeege answered, pulling the girls away from the door. "Come, missies, down ye go."

"Wait," Kimberly said, pulling her arm from Squeege as Abigail dug her heels in and refused to be led away. "She's trying to tell us something. I think it has something to do with the—"

Abigail pointed down into the water, and Kimberly nodded. "The whales. She wants to tell us something about the whales."

"What?" Squeege snapped, irritation showing in his red face.

Confused, Kimberly looked at Abigail, who pointed with a trembling hand toward the horizon and the steadily advancing ship.

"I know she likes the whales," Captain Blade said, obviously taking pains to keep his voice smooth. "She's been up here before, writing me notes about not killing the whales. Well, don't worry, miss, I told you we're not

77

whalers. Let Captain Moab do what he wishes, but we won't bother the animals."

Abigail shook her head so violently that Kimberly feared she would injure her neck. "She doesn't want Captain Moab to hurt them," Kimberly guessed. "Right, Abigail?"

Abigail pointed toward the reefed sails and made a downward pulling motion. Then she pointed again to the whales, and swung her arm out to sea.

"You want us to make sail?" Captain Blade guessed. "But we're in a dead calm. And if we leave, who will help your whale friends? They'll be sitting here, pretty as you please, for Captain Moab and his crew—"

Abigail shook her head and tugged on Blade's arm. Again she gestured to the whales, then swung her hands around and clasped them over her heart.

"I think she's trying to tell us that the whales like her," Kimberly said, scratching her head. "I could be wrong, but—"

Abigail grabbed Kimberly's hand and nodded energetically. Dumbfounded, Captain Blade looked toward his men, most of whom were entwined into the ship's rigging to catch a good view of the whales and the approaching ship. "Spread the canvas and make sail," he called upward, waving his hand above his head. "Show a leg there, and let's see what wind we can gather. Of certain 'twill do no harm to press on." He turned to the girls. "'Twill do no harm for ye to sponge off in a bucket of seawater, either. One of ye stinks to high heaven."

Squeege heard his captain's order and turned to bark the commands. "Away aloft! All hands ahoy! All hands to make sail!" The seamen cast off the lines that held the sails tightly furled to the yards and gathered the canvas under their arms.

"Let fall," came Squeege's order. "Sheet home. Look

alive. We're going to outrun the *Orca Blue*, so if ye are better men than her crew, now's the time to prove it!"

The *Seven Brothers* spread her wings like a graceful eagle. Beaming with joy, Abigail threw her arms around her friend before Kimberly had a chance to hold her nose.

* * *

Abigail went meekly below while the seamen spread the sails. Praying for a wind, she sat at the window and watched as the square sails of the *Orca Blue* grew larger and more pronounced on the horizon. God had answered her first prayer. If he was good, he would spare the whales. If he was merciful, he would send a wind. If he could truly do miracles, he would convince the whales to follow the *Seven Brothers*. And if he could do all those things, Abigail knew she could trust him the way Kimberly did—with her life.

The ship was effectively underway with a brisk wind before a quarter of an hour had passed. A run of living water sang at her side, and Angel, Cailin, and the other whales followed in the white swirling wake. It was the most beautiful sight Abigail had ever seen. The brilliant sea, darker blue than the sky, kept drawing her eyes away from the needle and canvas in her hands toward the mysterious wonders following the ship.

She would have thought the miracle complete had not the sails of the *Orca Blue* remained steadfast in the distance.

79

11

The dawn had spread a thick gray light over the quiet waters when Abigail awoke the next morning, and her first thought was for Angel, Cailin, and the other whales. They had still been with the ship when she fell asleep, but when she cast her eyes around the waters, she saw nothing. The whales had disappeared.

Not so Captain Moab. The coming sun revealed that the *Orca Blue* had caught the same wind that spurred the *Seven Brothers* forward. The whaling ship lay only a few yards off the starboard bow. Captain Moab was a persistent sailor, and apparently he was hoping that Captain Blade would again prove willing to lend a few of his seamen for the work of hunting the ocean's whales.

The children did not have to wonder about either captain's intentions for long. Soon after sunrise, Captain Blade sent Squeege and another sailor in the shallop to call upon Captain Moab. Abigail could hear the men's conversation easily in the still morning hours. After greeting each other in friendly tones, Squeege said he spoke for Captain Blade and asked why the *Orca Blue* persisted in following the *Seven Brothers*. "Can it be that y'are planning to follow us to Virginia?" he joked. "If ye keep up this shadowing of our ship—"

"I'll not be going to Virginia," Captain Moab answered, his voice punctuated by easy laughter. "'Tis only that I've noticed that the whales have taken a liking to your vessel. These are pilot whales, you know. They choose a leader and will follow him even to the death, if he should accidentally lead them into the shallows or into a pack of killer whales."

Squeege scratched his head. "So?"

"Well," Moab answered, a grin lighting up his dark face. "I'm beginning to think that these whales have adopted your ship as their leader since we killed the big brute who led them before. They are following ye, or haven't ye noticed? So, until I've taken my fill of them, I'll just lie low and wait for the whales to come home. I won't be a bother to ye and have no need of your men unless ye'd like to send some over—"

"Captain Blade says we're not whalers," Squeege answered with brittle dignity. "We're on our way to Virginia, and we intend to make good time. So we'll be continuing westward. We wish ye success and godspeed on your journey."

"Thank you," Captain Moab said, sweeping his hat toward the *Seven Brothers*, where Captain Blade waited on deck.

Abigail felt a sudden chill as she considered Moab's words. Was it possible that by calling out to the whales she had confused them? Did they really think this ship was another whale? Was it possible that *she* was their leader?

She was tempted to go again to the orlop deck and

cry out to the whales to warn them from the area. But if they misunderstood and came close as they had before, she'd be leading them right into a trap. Captain Moab and his ship would be waiting.

Stitching furiously, she jabbed her iron needle into her thumb, then burst into tears. It wasn't the pain that made her cry—it was the thought of how she may have led her whales to certain destruction.

* * *

"Whales ho!"

Kimberly closed her eyes as the cry echoed over the deck. Poor Abigail. She'd been so frantic to lead the whales away from the whalers' ship, and her plan had actually worked for most of a day and a night. But the *Orca Blue* spread more canvas than the *Seven Brothers* and was a swifter ship. And now the whales were coming again, right into the waters where Captain Moab had already lowered three whaleboats loaded with harpoons, lines, and men.

She cast a quick glance toward Abigail. The silent girl sat alone on the floor near the window, the same spot where she'd been sitting for hours. The mute girl's pain was clearly written on her face. Her green eyes were glassy and glittered strangely in the paleness of her complexion. Blood smeared her hand and stained the canvas in her lap.

At the sound of the lookout's cry, the children of the *Seven Brothers* rushed to the window to watch the whales. Kimberly stared in a paralysis of astonishment when the animals came directly into the space between the *Seven Brothers* and the waiting *Orca Blue*. Even the whalers were surprised by the whales' apparent indifference to the whaleboats and harpoons. Sly grins of expectation spread over their faces. "This will be easy," she heard one of the whalers call to his captain. "Like spearing fish in a barrel!"

"Daft creatures," Squeege muttered overhead. "Why'd they come back? Some say they are intelligent, but I'm having me doubts at this moment, I can tell ye."

The pod of whales came in close enough for Kimberly to see the light-colored area of skin that appeared like a saddle just behind the tall fins on their backs. They dove and rose again, chirping excitedly at each other and the children. The whalers watched, their harpoons resting lightly on their knees, their mouths open with delight at their good fortune.

"Well, what are we waitin' for?" Captain Moab called, his voice lively. "Set about, men, and get to work. Don't waste your time with the little 'uns today, but go for the nice big ones here. Get me that whale," he called, and Kimberly uttered an indrawn gasp when she realized he was pointing directly at the mother whale who swam with her baby.

"Aye, Captain," the foreman of the first whaleboat called. He braced himself in the narrow bow of the boat as his oarsmen began to row toward the mother. The whale raised her head above water, one dark eye fixed upon them, then swam to put herself between the approaching whaleboat and her baby. The front man raised his weapon, paused a moment to steady his aim, and let the harpoon fly.

84

The black, watchful eye of the mother whale blinked as the harpoon glanced off her thick skin, then she rolled her eyes back like an angry horse and opened her mouth with a terrible roar. Instantly, the pod dove for cover under the water, and the mother whale turned to face the whaleboat straight on. The flustered harpooner went pale as his hands furiously tried to pull in the rope attached to the useless harpoon. The charging whale was nearly upon the hapless crew when a second boat, creeping up from behind, sent a harpoon whizzing through the air. This lance pierced the thick, bulbous head of the mother. She

squealed and dove straight down, leaving nothing behind
but a flat space of ocean.

* * *

Angel's scream of pain chilled Abigail to the marrow, and
she flew to the window to watch the horror unfold. The
line attached to the harpoon hummed as it played out
over the edge of the boat, and the confident grins on the
whalers' faces faded when they realized that the mother
whale was taking more rope than they had to give.

"She can't be diving so far down," one of the whalers
said, his face a mask of disbelief. "There's two hundred
feet of line in that bucket."

"There *was* two hundred feet," another man
answered. "There's naught left but—"

In a flash, the rope ran out. The knotted end
snagged the narrow slot at the bow, and the whaleboat
pitched forward into the water. Her crew of six spilled
into the roiling sea, and the boat disappeared into the
deep as if it had been pulled under by some giant hand.

The third whaleboat set about the rescue of their
mates, and Abigail turned her attention to Captain Moab
on the deck of the *Orca Blue*. Couldn't he see that Angel
was no ordinary whale? Mayhap he would leave her alone
now that she had sunk one of his whaleboats—

But no. "I've never seen a whale dive so fast, nor so
far," he called to his men. "But she will have to come up
for air, and soon. Fan out, all of you, and find that whale.
A whale that can dive like that will have blubber to spare,
and that means more oil for each of us. Don't let her get
away!"

More whaleboats splashed into the sea. The wet
survivors of the first lost boat were quickly transferred
to new ones, and the whaleboats fanned out to wait for
Angel to surface. Abigail leaned forward and scanned the

85

waters for a sign of Cailin. Angel had been protecting her, so it was likely the little whale still lingered in the area.

A sharp bleating cry suddenly pricked Abigail's sensitive ears. The timbers of the ship seemed to vibrate with it, and instantly Abigail knew from whom and where the sound had come. *Cailin was hiding under the ship!*

"Mama whale's been down five minutes," one of the men called.

"No whale can stay down longer than ten," Moab answered. "And if she's hurt, she won't last nearly so long. Don't let her slip up on you, mates."

The men in the whaleboats steadied themselves in their narrow skiffs. The front men, each holding a harpoon, braced themselves with one upraised knee while they peered nervously into the restless water.

"Hey, Captain," one of the men called up. "Didn't that whale have a baby? Mayhap if we spear the small one, the big one will come in a hurry. I've seen it happen time and again."

"You're right," Moab answered. "Find the little one."

Quietly, expertly, the whaleboats paddled until they had made a wide circle surrounding the area between the two larger vessels. Abigail heard muffled comments from the deck of her own ship and knew that Captain Blade was not happy about this invasion of his sea space. His men were readying the sails now, eager to be off, but if he pulled out and left Cailin defenseless . . .

A small blast of air sounded from the water outside her window, and Abigail looked straight down. Cailin hovered there, hiding in the shadows cast by the *Seven Brothers*'s bow. Abigail could see her, alone and dark in the water, waiting for her mother to return. Unfortunately, the sound that had alerted Abigail to her presence had called the whalers too.

"There!" one of them shouted, and a whaleboat turned and began to move toward Cailin. She squealed and dove, but the whalers kept coming, knowing that the little whale would have to surface again soon. "We'll harpoon the baby and drag it behind us," the front man explained to his crew. "That will bring the mother whale out of hiding. She's out there now, waiting to see what we will do."

From his place at the windows, Ethan raised his arm and pointed out to the water. "Look there!" he cried, his voice quivering. "Isn't that a—"

"A shark," Thatcher finished, his eyes studying the silvery gray fin that sliced through the water. "He smells blood. The mother whale is wounded."

"She must be near," Kimberly said, her voice rising in excitement.

"I see others," Wingate said, waving his hand over the sea. "Look, the sharks are coming faster now."

Abigail blocked their conversation from her mind and concentrated upon the whaleboat just a few feet away outside the window. She knew how Cailin felt. She was alone, frightened, and in danger, afraid to make a sound, afraid to breathe, wondering where her mother had gone. Like she had felt when Lizabeth left her.

A dark surface loomed through the water near the ship, and Abigail held her breath. The harpooner saw it, too, and motioned for his crew to row closer. He was sure this was the baby whale, for no other animal had this long and slender shape. The harpooner leaned forward and raised his weapon; Cailin crested the top of a wave and her blowhole opened explosively for a much-needed gulp of air.

Abigail decided to act. She would help Cailin, no matter what the cost.

"Noooooo!" she screamed, leaping out the window.

12

Kimberly felt the hairs lift on her arms as Abigail threw back her head and let loose a shriek no one there would soon forget. Suddenly Abigail's kirtle was billowing about her as she flew out the window, and the resulting splash startled every man and child aboard both ships. As Kimberly peered down, she saw Abigail rise from the deep, her long red hair streaming behind her, her arms and legs thrashing in the water. "Hang on, missy!" Squeege called from above, and the seamen exploded into action as they hurried to lower the shallop.

"Why doesn't one of them jump in and save her?" Kimberly cried, watching as Abigail disappeared beneath the waves.

"The sharks," Wingate answered, pointing to the fins circling not far from where Abigail had disappeared.

A wave seemed to bring Abigail to the surface, and Kimberly saw her struggle upward and gasp for breath, then she slipped beneath the water again. "Hurry," Kimberly cried, beating her hands on the rough wood of the window. "She'll drown."

"Look," Ethan said, pointing toward a sharp fin veering toward Abigail. "They're closing in."

"Dear God," Kimberly whispered, closing her eyes in a frantic prayer. "Help her. Keep the sharks away."

As Kimberly opened her eyes, Abigail's head, shoulders, and arms rose from the deep. Every child on the ship gasped in surprise at the strange sight before them, and a great exultation filled Kimberly's chest until she thought it would burst. *Abigail is riding a whale!* She sat astride the whale, her hands clutching the tall fin on the creature's back, her legs straddling the light-colored patch of skin that had reminded Kimberly of a saddle. Most amazing, Abigail seemed to be crooning to the baby whale. As if in obedience to her command, the whale swam away from the area between the two ships and headed for open sea.

The click of a musket broke the silence of fascination. "Ye men will drop your harpoons," Captain Blade's voice called, ringing with authority. "Ye will not strike at any whale as long as the child remains in the water. Put your harpoons away."

Kimberly held tight to the windowsill and leaned forward to look out the window. The baby whale turned once it left the immediate area between the ships and seemed to be cruising slowly along the surface, keeping Abigail's head clearly above water. Squeege and his crew had thrown their rope ladders over the side and were now climbing into the shallop to rescue her.

"I don't know why ye need more convincing than this," Captain Blade continued, and from his shadow on the water Kimberly could see that he still aimed his musket at the deck of the *Orca Blue.* "But ye will take no whales today. Haul in your men and your boats, Captain

Moab, and leave us to our journey." Moab shook his head as if to wake himself from a dream, but then he gave the order to call in his boats.

Around Kimberly, the other children stood in stunned silence. Brooke was quietly crying. Ethan stared at the circling sharks with a worried frown. Thatcher leaned against a post, a fascinated and curious expression on his face. Several of the younger children were disturbed and whispered to one another.

Joshua looked up at Kimberly with honest fear in his eyes and asked if Abigail had been swallowed by the whale like Jonah. "Nay, she hasn't," Kimberly said, dropping her hand on the small boy's head. "But the same God who protected Jonah will protect our Abigail. Wait and see."

* * *

Abigail sat in the shallop, shivering but elated by her wild ride through the ocean. More than once she had run her hand over Cailin's slippery skin to reassure herself that she wasn't dreaming. The whale's skin was cool and smooth beneath her, her swimming gentle and considerate as she carried Abigail away from the circling sharks and the harpoons of the whalers.

Abigail had been almost reluctant to catch the rope Squeege threw to her from the safety of the shallop, but common sense reminded her that she couldn't swim in the ocean forever. Cailin probably couldn't remain on the surface for long, either, because the sun's hot rays were already beginning to dry her skin. So Abigail caught the rope and allowed the sailors to pull her into the shallop while she cried out her whale noises. Cailin chirped in response before diving and disappearing from sight.

As they rowed back to the *Seven Brothers*, Abigail was pleased to see that the *Orca Blue* had begun to hoist her

91

whaleboats aboard. But still she worried about Angel. She had been injured—that was obvious from the number of sharks circling in the area. But where had she gone?

* * *

A quarter of an hour later, once the shallop and its occupants had been taken safely back aboard the ship, Abigail heard Kimberly cry out and point toward the sea. "Look there! Isn't that the mother whale?"

Abigail dropped the sheet of canvas Squeege had given her for a blanket and sprinted toward the window. Angel had returned, along with several other large whales. They churned up the sea just to the east of the two ships and seemed to be waiting for something.

"What are they doing?" Brooke asked, turning to Abigail.

Abigail shook her head.

Suddenly, in a determined rush, the pod of whales directed their energy toward the *Orca Blue*. Swimming furiously toward Captain Moab's ship, they rammed it with their huge, pot-shaped heads. The first few blows did no real damage and only sent the bewildered crew scurrying to the rail. In the second assault, however, one particularly hard blow sent a sailor running to the captain. From where they watched, the children could hear his frightened cry: "We've sprung a leak below the waterline, Captain. I can't repair it unless you get us out of these waters, for another blow will surely rupture the wall."

Captain Moab needed no urging. "Make sail!" he bellowed, turning to his deck crew. "Sheet home every sail! All hands to make sail on the double!"

The men of the *Orca Blue* sprang into action, and the children cheered as the sailors scurried over the rigging like frightened rats. Within minutes, the ship began to pull away from the *Seven Brothers*, and at the first sign of the ship's retreat, the furious assault of the whales ceased.

But they did not swim away. Angel swam forward to comfort Cailin, and when they both surfaced in unison near the ship, Abigail saw that Angel had managed to extract the harpoon from her forehead. A tiny slice remained there, but it would heal in time.

Abigail shivered in her wet clothes. "We should get you out of those things," Brooke said, coming over with the sheet of canvas in her hands. "Wrap yourself in this, and let me spread your blouse and kirtle on the window-sill to dry." She gave Abigail a teasing smile. "You did yourself a favor, Abigail, by dousing your clothes in salt water. Mayhap when they're dried they won't stink."

While Brooke held up the canvas as a screen, Abigail slipped out of her wet clothes. Maybe they did smell bad, but she'd never again smell bad breath without smiling and thinking of the whales. And she'd never think of the whales, or the ocean, or this ship without remembering how God had worked to spare Angel and Cailin because she asked him to. If God cared enough about two creatures of the deep to work a miracle, then he surely cared about her. And she'd never, ever forget that.

93

* * *

Glad to be rid of the dark ship that had shadowed him, Captain Blade ordered the *Seven Brothers'* sails spread immediately. The whales remained with the ship for about an hour, Kimberly guessed, then they dove together and swam northward in a staggered single line. "Such power," she said, watching them go. "The way they tore into Captain Moab's ship—I wouldn't have believed it unless I saw it myself."

"Such control," Wingate answered. "Did you see how gentle the baby whale was with Abigail? And how tender the mother was with her baby? She has great power to defend her calf, but she has great meekness with her friends."

He paused as if he wanted to say something more, and Kimberly looked at him. Wingate was her friend, but she had been harsh with him in the last few days. She'd been harsh with everyone, frustrated by the young ones, annoyed that no one listened to her lessons or stories.

"I'm sorry," she whispered, leaning on her elbows as she looked out the window. "I guess lately I've been acting more like the mother whale in a rage. I thought that no one would listen to me unless I was angry."

"Anger has its place," Wingate said. "But gentleness should be our first response. I think you can be gentle and still teach the others, Kimberly. Your mother was gentle, just like the mother whale. Gentleness wins more friends than harshness."

His words stung, but Kimberly accepted them quietly. Wingate was right. She had not been gentle, and she needed to tell her friends that she was truly sorry.

Clearing her throat, she walked to the mainmast to make her announcement and her apology.

* * *

Abigail wrapped the sailcloth more tightly about her and rubbed her hand over its surface. If given enough of it, she could make suitable outfits for some of the little ones whose clothes were wearing away. It was a strong fabric, and water-repellent.

"Abigail." Brooke and Wingate stood before her, and Abigail blushed because she hadn't seen them coming.

"You spoke, you know, when you jumped out of the window," Wingate said, his face bright with eagerness. "We thought mayhap you would like to try speaking again."

Abigail blushed and looked at the floor. She hadn't thought about speaking when she jumped to help Cailin;

the sound had come from her almost by itself. But if she had to think about making the right sounds to communicate her thoughts, she'd surely mess everything up. And they would all laugh because they thought talking was so *easy*—

"If you're worried about people laughing at you," Brooke said, guessing her thoughts, "we won't let them."

"Why should anyone laugh at you?" Wingate said, moving closer. "Why, you're the only girl I know who can talk to *whales!* You have a talent far beyond anyone else's. So, if you want to try to speak to people, too—"

"We'd be glad to help," Brooke said. "You can count on us. Whenever you're ready, Abigail, just let us know. We think you can do it."

"You don't want to remain silent forever, do you?" Wingate asked.

Abigail smiled and pressed her lips together. "No," she said, a blush of pleasure rising to her cheeks

WEEK
FOUR

Wednesday, June 2, 1627

13

Only a smudge of sun dappled through the heavy cloud cover, and Kimberly crinkled her nose at the light as she peered through one of the ship's windows. She was grateful for the overcast sky. If the sun continued to shine as brightly as it had through the last days of their voyage, by the end of the summer she'd be as freckled as Abigail or as brown as Ethan's coffee-colored eyes.

From where she sat at one of the wide windows that opened to miles of endless ocean, Kimberly could hear the soft lap of waves brushing against the ship, the sound of children talking and laughing, and the thundering footsteps of the crew on the deck above. The children weren't allowed on the uppermost deck unless expressly granted permission by Captain Blade, but Kimberly noticed that lately Thatcher Butler was frequently invited up to lend the seamen a hand. Maybe, Kimberly mused, the captain planned to purchase Thatcher himself once they reached

Virginia. She knew Thatcher would enjoy a life of service on the open sea, but the thought of never seeing him in Jamestown made her feel strangely sad.

Kimberly crossed her legs and modestly tucked her kirtle around her knees. A group of half a dozen younger children sat in front of her, earnestly tracing the letters *a*, *b*, and *c* on the wide wooden planks of the flooring. There was but one lump of coal that Kimberly used to write letters and words on the dark floor, and she had to make that last for the journey, so Kimberly taught the alphabet by asking the children to use their fingers as imaginary pens. She had assured the young ones that their lives in Virginia would be far better if they could read and write, so they worked hard.

Joshua, the blond boy who usually had a mischievous gleam in his eye, stuck his tongue out of the corner of his mouth as he concentrated on his work. Kimberly smothered a smile with her hand. She was proud of her young students and wouldn't want them to think she was laughing at them.

Across the hold, Wingate and Abigail were trying to teach several of the others how to run a rope through the edge of a sail and whipstitch the bent edge into place. Abigail made dull, flat sounds as she worked, mimicking the speech of the others. By common agreement, the other children ignored her stuttering, repetitious noises. Kimberly and Brooke had explained that if Abigail was to speak, she would have to practice.

Brooke with Denni and Daryl, French twins who had been aboard the ship when it docked in London. Denni and Daryl had only been able to say "Shall we eat yet?" when Kimberly first came aboard, but they now had a passable command of the English language, thanks to Brooke's patient tutoring. "I never thought my French lessons would be of any use," Brooke told Kimberly one afternoon. "And just look what good I'm doing here!"

"Denni and Daryl will appreciate your help even more when they are sold to a master and mistress," Kimberly said, a shadow falling over her heart as she thought of the future all the other children would face. For whether they had been kidnapped or came willingly aboard the *Seven Brothers*, the money for their overseas passage would come from their sale into indentured service. And as Kimberly often reminded them, the best-educated and most-skilled children would find themselves working in the houses and merchant shops at Jamestown. Those who could not read nor write, or who proved disagreeable, would find themselves pulling weeds under a blazing sun in the tobacco fields.

Thank God there will be no indentured service for me, Kimberly thought; then a wave of guilt passed over her. If the grace of God had not allowed her and her mother to pay for their overseas passage, she would be facing indenture herself. But even though her father waited for her in Virginia, because her mother had died scarcely a week after their journey had begun Kimberly often felt as alone and abandoned as the others.

Christian, a homeless orphan who had neither sight nor a last name, leaned against the mainmast, quietly humming a familiar English tune. And Ethan sat at the starboard window, looking out to sea. She thought he was saying his prayers, for Ethan was as devout and religious a person as anyone she had ever met. He was Jewish, and although Kimberly wasn't exactly sure how her beliefs differed from his, she was determined that one day she'd pull him aside and have a long talk with him.

The easy, relaxed sound of laughter rose from another group of children at the rear of the ship, and Kimberly leaned against the broad beams of the ship's wall and smiled. In just three weeks, through danger, adventure, and trouble, the captives had become a sort of family. Except for Captain Blade, who had his own small

101

cabin, it was nearly impossible for anyone to find himself totally alone on the ship. Given the extreme closeness of their situation, the children had come to accept one another like brothers and sisters. The occasional squabble still broke out, and feelings were hurt as tempers flared. But when quarreling children had to live, eat, sleep, and breathe only a few feet away from each other, they usually learned to make allowances for imperfections. And when the younger children misbehaved, Kimberly and the older ones were quick to impose justice and order.

"We'll make it yet, Mama," she whispered, then her throat closed as an overwhelming sadness rose from her heart. Her mother had been gone for two weeks now, yet Kimberly still found herself thinking, *Oh, Mama would like that*, and *I'll have to tell Mama about this*.

She bit her lip as tears filled her eyes. Despite her resolve not to grieve, an inner loneliness remained with her. "I guess that's why you created heaven, Lord," she whispered. She dashed the tears from her eyes and made an effort to smile at her young students. It wasn't good to think too much about her loss. She had too much time for thinking on this journey and not enough things to do. She spent much of the morning teaching her lessons to the younger children, but the afternoons stretched before her like an empty canvas—and they were still several weeks away from Virginia!

Kimberly blew out her cheeks. What would she be doing if she were home in London? She and her mother had spent most days working in Master Walker's pie shop, but after the sun set they'd go home to their tiny rooms and eat supper together. After a quiet meal of bread and cheese, Kimberly's mother would take down her Bible and open it on her lap. Spreading out its rustling pages with her thin hand, she would begin to read aloud while Kimberly knitted or worked with her needle.

The lump rose again to Kimberly's throat. What

she'd give to have her mother's Bible now! But it had been packed into a trunk and left on a dock in London. As far as she knew, no one aboard the ship had a copy of the Bible. The other children had no bags or trunks at all, and the bilge boys who lived below owned nothing but the shirts and breeches they wore. But surely one of the sailors had a Bible! It would be so wonderful to read it during the afternoons, and she could teach lessons to the younger children.

Someone had to have a Bible. And if such a one believed in God, he wouldn't mind letting Kimberly borrow it.

She stood and swayed for a moment with the ship, then went to ask the other children if perchance they had a Bible tucked into a pocket.

* * *

"Baruch atah Adonai, Eloheinu melech ha-olam," Ethan Reis whispered so no one else could hear. *Blessed are you, O Lord, our God, King of the universe. If you are King of the universe, couldn't you have prevented the terrible thing that has happened to me? 'Twould not have been so difficult to keep my footsteps close to my parents. But I stopped at the docks to stare at the jellyfish that you, O Lord, placed in the water, and when I looked up, my father, mother, and sister were gone. We were traveling on a boat from Spain, bound for Germany, and were only going to stop in England for a short time. But you, O Lord, caused my feet to slow and stumble. And when the men offered to help me find my parents, how was I to know that their hearts were evil? For they brought me to this ship, and not to my mother and father, and now I am truly a stranger bound for a strange land where the inhabitants do not know you.*

His heart went down, sinking into a deep pool of sorrow. He and his family had lived in a tightly knit Jewish community while in Spain, and rarely did Ethan

103

have contact or communication with the Gentile world. With friends and kinsmen, his family celebrated the weekly Sabbath and sang the *z'mirot*, songs of praise to God. People ate, talked, and prayed at his family's generous dinner table. The delicious meals prepared by his mother were never hurried, and when they were finally finished, everyone joined in to sing the *bentshen*, the after-meal prayer that expressed gratitude for the sustenance they had received. The Jewish feasts of Passover, Pentecost, and Purim were part of an endless cycle into which Ethan had been born, and he had expected to continue observing the festivals and feasts with his family and friends until he was an old man. He would teach the songs and stories to his sons the way his father had taught him . . . or would he? How could he sing the Sabbath songs in a strange land and with strange people? And what would his father do without him?

His father was a learned man who spoke Spanish, Hebrew, German, and English with equal ease. Ethan and his sister, Sarah, had been taught all four languages, and since the earliest days of his childhood Ethan had been schooled in the study of the Talmud, the Jews' holy writings.

104   While his father had been firm, his mother had been soft and generous. She was a beautiful woman, with hair that flowed down onto her shoulders in a soft dark tide and eyes that shone gold in the light of the Sabbath candles. Even now Ethan could close his eyes and hear her Sabbath blessing in the voice of the wind: *Shabbat Shalom, my beloved son. Sabbath peace to you.*

His sister, Sarah, was two years younger than Ethan. Because she was nine and always gawking at the unusual and unfamiliar, his parents had held both her hands that day as they walked along the docks at the London shipyard. Ethan, as the older child, was left to follow.

And in that he had failed. Now he was lost forever

on a ship where no one understood him. Kimberly Hollis seemed very kind and sympathetic, but she couldn't speak Hebrew. She only stared at him in confusion when he tried to explain the meaning and reason behind his Hebrew prayers. She claimed to worship the same God that he did, but she spoke often of Jesus, and Ethan knew that name had made both of his parents shudder. And yet something in Ethan's soul stirred to know more of this man.

Early Jewish literature referred to Jesus as "the Man" without mentioning his name, as if it were too horrible to pen onto paper. The Talmud taught that Jesus was an impostor, a truly wicked man, a sorcerer, idolater, and a false tempter. Once Ethan heard a great teacher say that Christianity was the invention of an ugly little Jew by the name of Paul, a man who suffered from epileptic seizures and often hallucinated. Jesus himself, the teacher said, was an embarrassment to the Jews of his day because he threatened to cause trouble with the Romans. The Jewish leaders took him into custody to protect him from himself and finally surrendered him to the Romans, who crucified him.

So why hadn't this man's name disappeared from the face of the earth? Other men had come and gone through the portals of time, other Jews had risen up and claimed to be the true Messiah. And yet the name of one Jew, Jesus, lingered on every tongue in the Gentile world.

Ethan shivered. "May his name be blotted out, and his memory," he muttered, hoping the words would have the power to keep dark thoughts away.

105

14

Kimberly carried out her search through the children's hold and in the lower hold with the bilge boys, and then climbed up the companionway and timidly asked Squeege for permission to talk to the seamen on the upper deck. "What is it you're wanting?" the bosun asked, thrusting his meaty hands onto his hips. "I'll not have you bothering the men for some silly thing—"

"I want a Bible," she said, her voice quiet.

The frown vanished from Squeege's face. "Aye, and so you should," he said, nodding. "Well, I don't think any of the men have got one, for none of 'em can read. The captain reads, of course, and he has the *Book of Common Prayer*—is that what you're wanting?"

"Nay," Kimberly answered, shaking her head. "I want a regular Bible, just like the one my mother used to read—Genesis through Revelation. Will you ask the sailors for me, Squeege?"

"Aye," the bosun promised, nodding.

Kimberly lowered the trapdoor and slipped back into the hold, her spirits sinking. How could it be that not one person aboard would have the *Holy Bible!* Why, King James himself had commissioned a new translation of the Scriptures so that even the common people could read and understand the Word of God.

An hour later Squeege lifted the hatch and peered down into the hold. "Sorry," he said, his eyes meeting Kimberly's. "No man up here has a copy of the Scriptures. And Captain Blade has only his prayer book."

"Oh," Kimberly said, her shoulders drooping. "Thank you for asking about it, Squeege."

The trapdoor dropped into place with a muffled boom, and Kimberly chewed her thumbnail. Where could she get a Bible? Certain portions of the Scriptures would be in the captain's prayer book, so that would make a good start, and she had memorized other passages of her favorite Scriptures. . . .

"Wingate," she called, gesturing for him to come near. "I have an important question to ask you."

"Yea?" Wingate said, his brows slanting in curiosity. He walked over and sat on the floor next to Kimberly. "What do you want to know?"

Thatcher, who'd been eavesdropping as always, leaned toward Kimberly. "Yea, what do you want to know?" he asked, mimicking Wingate's tone. "If Wingate does not know what you're asking, mayhap I will."

"I doubt it," Kimberly said dryly. She pressed one finger to her lips for a moment, then pointed at Wingate. "If all the Bibles in the world were destroyed and we had to rewrite the holy Scriptures from what we know in our heads, how much could you write?"

Wingate broke into a lopsided grin. "Are you joking? Surely you can think of someone better to ask than me. I haven't heard a Bible reading since my mother died." He scratched his head. "Hold a minute—the rector at the church where we got free soup often muttered a bit of the Scriptures as he doled out our dinner. Mayhap I could remember a line or two."

"I might know a wee bit," Thatcher inserted.

Both Kimberly and Wingate looked at him in surprise.

Thatcher shrugged. "I know that Jesus worked to clean the streets."

"Where in the world did you hear that?" Kimberly asked.

Thatcher let out a short laugh touched with embarrassment. "'Tis in the Bible, I'd bet me life on it. It says as plain as day: 'Jesus swept.'"

Kimberly nearly choked on her laughter while Wingate threw back his head in a loud guffaw. "That's 'Jesus wept,' you knave," he said, slapping his hand upon his knee. "Even I know that."

"I don't know what kind of Bible we'd put together if we relied on the likes of you two," Kimberly said, an idea slowly germinating within her. "But mayhap the others have a clearer recollection of God's Word than you do. And if we put our minds to it, we just might be able to come up with a passable set of Scriptures, at least enough to last till we get to Virginia."

109

"I say 'twill be nothing but folly to try," Wingate warned, wiping tears of laughter from his eyes.

"But it will give us something to do," Kimberly answered. "And my mother always said that the Word of God is like honey to the soul. After the troubles we've seen in the past few days, mayhap we could all use a little sweetness in our lives."

* * *

At length darkness fell upon the ship. Through the embracing folds of sleep Ethan murmured his evening prayers and dreamed of home and his parents. "Be proud of who you are," his father's deep voice suddenly rumbled, and Ethan saw him sitting at the family dinner table, his hands folded for prayer, his dark eyes intent upon Ethan's face. "You are one of the chosen people. Though we have suffered much according to the design of the Master of the universe, even so we have been greatly blessed."

"How, Father?" Ethan asked, thinking of the Gentile schoolboys who had taunted him as he walked home from his yeshiva, his Jewish school. He hadn't felt at all blessed when a rock they threw cut him on the forehead.

"We are blessed because we follow the principles of God," his father answered, crossing his arms. His dark, deeply wrinkled eyes studied Ethan from beneath thick brown brows. Those glittering eyes seemed to have found the answers to the world's most difficult questions, and Ethan always felt his stomach turn over whenever they fastened upon him. "I remember Aaron of Lincoln," his father said, slowly scratching his dark brown beard. "England, where we will travel soon, was a financial mess during the twelfth century. But by following the financial principles of the Talmud, Aaron of Lincoln amassed a fortune of such magnitude that all of England's nobles and churchmen were in his debt. When Aaron died, the king took over his assets, and the sum involved was so great that a special branch of the royal treasury had to be set up to manage all the people who had owed money to Aaron of Lincoln."

"I have heard about this," Ethan said slowly, lowering his eyes from his father's passionate stare. He remembered other taunts from Gentile boys. "Some say Jews want to take everyone's money."

"Bah." His father waved the words away. "Whether they are Jew or Gentile, successful bankers are wise and make good investments. But Jews have other talents, my son. Years before Christopher Columbus sailed from

110

Spain, Jews disproved the notion that the world is flat. The ancient Midrash tells us that the world is shaped like a ball thrown from the hand. And in the Zohar 'tis written that the earth revolves like a sphere so that it is day on one half of the world and night on the other."

Ethan nodded slowly. He had studied the ancient texts as he learned to read.

"Without the help of Bagriel Sanchez, Juan Cabero, and Luis de Santangel, all Jewish counselors to the king of Spain," his father went on, "Columbus would not have ever left Spain to discover the New World. And when we sail to England, our captain will certainly use maps drawn by Jewish mapmakers. Even the sea quadrant used for navigation was invented by Levi ben Gershon, another Jew."

Ethan did not answer. It was not wise to interrupt his father while he was teaching.

"But oh, my son, how we have suffered. The Pharaoh in Egypt tried to exterminate our forefathers. Nebuchadnezzar deported Jews. Haman tried to wipe us from the face of the earth. The Romans leveled our holy city. Constantine outlawed Jews. England imprisoned our people and took our wealth before we were expelled from England altogether. The Spanish Inquisition has tortured our people and killed them, and even Switzerland and Germany have persecuted us. Those who call themselves Christians have herded our people into ghettos to keep us far away from them. But still, we have flourished. The hand of God is upon us, my son, and he has promised to bless those who bless us and curse those who curse us. Listen to my words, Son, and learn."

"Will it always be this way?" Ethan asked, squinting as the image of his father quivered and dimmed.

"All persecution will end when our Messiah comes." His father's voice was still firm. "The Scriptures tell us that our Messiah is coming, a descendent of Abraham and

David, a Savior and a Sovereign. He will live a perfect life and reign over the world in righteousness and honor. Evil will be vanquished, and our sins will be forever wiped away by his power. We look forward to this day, my son, and we pray for his soon appearance. You must always pray for the Messiah to come, and you must never forget who you are."

The dark eyes seemed to glow with an inner fire as Ethan's father spoke. "The story is told of a Jew who was driven from Spain with his family. At sea he lost the few possessions he had remaining, and his children and wife were carried off by pirates. But that man stood upon his feet, spread his hands heavenward, and cried, 'Master of the universe! Much hast thou done to me to make me abandon my faith. Yet know thou of a certainty that a Jew I am and a Jew I will remain.'"

The glittering eyes focused on Ethan and held him tightly though the rest of the room swirled around him. "I know that you feel lost, my son, but you will never be alone as long as you remember who you are. You are a Jew, one of the chosen, and you must live as a Jew. Never forget this. You will be lost forever if you fail."

"I will not fail you, Father," Ethan cried, his heart 112 beating faster as his father's form and face vanished into a hazy mist. "Don't go!"

But there was no answer, and when Ethan forced his eyes to open, he was surrounded by darkness in the hold of the ship.

Thursday, June 3

15

Kimberly noticed that she was walking on tiptoe as she approached the companionway. *You're being silly*, she told herself, forcing herself to take a deep breath. *There is no reason to be afraid of Captain Blade. 'Tis true enough that he is a stern sort, not given to easy answers or frequent smiles, but he seems a fair-minded man and not the type to refuse a request such as this.*

"You're not going up, are you?" Wingate interrupted her concentration, and Kimberly pulled her foot off the narrow staircase as if it had burned her.

"Why not? I only want to ask the captain for a few sheets of parchment and a pen so we can write down the Scriptures."

"But you're going up without *permission*." Wingate shot her a half-frightened look. "You know the captain doesn't like us going up to the seamen's deck."

"Thatcher's been going up every day," Kimberly said

confidently, though she didn't feel certain enough to put her foot on the stair again. "And I think Captain Blade will understand why we need the parchment, Wingate. He seems like a man who fears God, so he'll agree that we need a copy of the Scriptures—"

"He's a kidnapper, Kimberly. Can you be forgetting that?"

"Is he?" she asked, raising an eyebrow as she turned to him.

Wingate frowned and thrust his hands into the air. "What do you mean? Of course he is! Who's piloting this ship and taking us from our homes—"

"If I remember aright, Wingate, you wanted to come on this ship," Kimberly said, lowering her voice. "And Thatcher actually volunteered for the journey."

"What about Brooke?" Wingate demanded in a harsh whisper. He glanced nervously about, and Kimberly guessed that he did not want to remind the others of experiences that ought to remain in the past. Brooke had not borne the separation from her home easily. "Our lady Brooke was stolen while her nanny's back was turned. And there are scores of others here who were snatched up from the streets—"

114

"I know," Kimberly snapped, cutting him off. She moved closer and lowered her voice further. "I know about the men who did the snatching. But Captain Blade wasn't among them, and I don't think he's the type to do such a thing. He's a man of the sea, and he was hired to captain this ship. I truly think that's the end of it."

"You do." Wingate's voice was flat, and he gazed at Kimberly with an air of disbelief. "Next I suppose you'll be telling me that the captain's a saint."

"He was very kind to my mother when she was ill," Kimberly said, folding her arms. "And he's never had a harsh word to say in my presence. I think you're misjudging him, that's all."

She lifted her chin and climbed the companionway with a show of courage she did not feel. Wingate stood below and stared upward as she rapped timidly on the hatch that covered the opening. When no one answered her knock, she smiled bravely and used both her hands to press upward until the trapdoor moved away.

Forgetting about Wingate, she climbed up another step until her head protruded out of the opening. "Mister Squeege!" she called, glancing round the upper deck. A half dozen sailors sat on casks in a line, each man combing out and plaiting the long hair of the sailor in front of him. At the sound of her voice, the sailors turned to stare at her, then they glanced away, apparently more willing to watch the sea than to bother with one of the children who made up the cargo of the *Seven Brothers*.

"Ahoy, missy! Stay there, and I'll be down directly!" Kimberly heard Squeege's call and looked up. He was twined in the rigging on the mainmast beside her, and he scampered downward with the ease of a man who knows no fear of heights.

Kimberly took advantage of the rare moment. The captives lived, ate, and slept in the bowels of the ship, and she had nearly forgotten how wonderful fresh air could feel. The wind up here was sweet, the air pungent with the smells of water and salt. Light scribbles of clouds passed overhead through a wide turquoise sky. The dazzling white blur of the sun stood fixed behind the stiffened, bloated sails, and the bowsprit dipped and rose again, sending a cool splash of spray into the air and over the deck. The upper deck was a relief from the crowded, smelly conditions of the lower hold, and it was worth risking the captain's anger just to enjoy a few minutes in the fresh air and sunlight.

"Now, what are you about, missy?" Squeege called,

jumping from the rigging. He landed as easily as a monkey on the planking in front of her, his bare feet slapping the floor. "I thought you understood that the captain doesn't want a swarm of youngsters on his deck."

"I only need one thing—well, two, actually," Kimberly said, playing her brightest smile upon the bosun. "A few sheets of parchment and a pen. And a bottle of ink, of course."

"That's three things," Squeege growled.

Kimberly tilted her head. "Ah, so 'tis. Well, do you think the captain will be willing to give them to us? 'Twould be a great relief to me to have these materials, for I know Captain Blade wants me to keep the children occupied. And if they're busy with the project I have planned, they won't be a bother to the captain at all."

"Project?" Squeege asked, raising a bushy brow. "What project are you thinkin' of?"

"We want to write out the Bible," Kimberly said, folding her hands neatly in front of her. "There's not a complete set of Scriptures on this entire ship, and 'tis a shame, that. Surely the captain will see that 'twill be an honor and a joy for us to write down whatever Scriptures we have hidden in our hearts, and the work will be beneficial to everyone. God will of certain smile on our efforts, Mister Squeege, and if God approves, surely the captain will, too."

She knew that her appeal had worked on Squeege, for the frown that had ridden his brow suddenly lifted. "Well now, missy," he said, squinting sideways at her. "Mayhap if I go to the captain with you and explain first, you know, to soften him up a bit—"

"Thank you, Squeege," Kimberly said, stepping out of the companionway onto the deck. She took another deep breath of the marvelous fresh air. "I'm sure the captain won't mind."

* * *

Below in the hold, Ethan sat with his back to the others and his face to the wall. He wanted to be alone with his thoughts and the memory of his dream, but Kimberly Hollis's voice floated down to him from the companionway. She wanted to write the Bible, she was telling Squeege. A wry smile flitted across Ethan's face. As if one person could write the Bible! He didn't know what sort of Bible the Christians used, but the Hebrew Talmud was a monstrously long work. The Torah, the basis of the Jewish Scriptures, could be written out in 350 pages, but it would take more than 523 *books* to hold the information contained in the Talmud.

But like every Jewish boy he knew, Ethan had studied the Talmud every day and committed long sections of it to memory. The study of the Torah was relatively simple. Moses had written these five books of the Law, and Ethan had always found them to be concise and to the point. But the Talmud was made up of other books that came after the Torah—books to explain the Torah, and then other books to explain the explanations. Ethan thought the Talmud was sometimes boring, sometimes clever, sometimes funny, sometimes wordy. In the pages of its books he found songs and sayings, fables and fancies, wisdom and wit. There were rules and more rules about how to keep the commandments first given in the Torah. Because God told his people to "remember the Sabbath day to keep it holy," one of the books in the Talmud spelled out forty kinds of work that were forbidden on the Sabbath. On the day of rest, a Jew could not untie a knot, sew two stitches, light a fire, or carry anything from one place to another. A Jew who observed the commandments could not suck on a piece of candy on the Sabbath unless he placed it in his mouth before the Sabbath began. If the candy fell out, he could not put it back into his mouth, for that would be work.

117

"What are you thinking about, Ethan?" a shy voice whispered, disturbing his thoughts.

Ethan turned around and met Brooke Burdon's blue eyes. She was blonde and fair, everything his mother and sister were not. For some reason, the girl's presence always left Ethan feeling uncomfortable.

But she sat down beside him, and Ethan shifted his weight. Couldn't she tell that he was not in a mood for conversation? And she was asking about his thoughts, which no Gentile could ever understand. He felt the distance between them like an open wound.

"I'm thinking about the ways of my people," he said quietly.

"What people?"

"The Jews."

Brooke's face was totally blank. "Who are the Jews? Are they gentle folk?"

Ethan sighed. How could he describe his ancient race to this pampered little princess? She thought in terms of English society, but his people had been spread throughout the world when England was still nothing but an uncivilized forest. "My people, the Jews, are the descendants of Abraham," he began, not looking at her. "We are the chosen race. From out of the children of Israel will come a Messiah, and on account of him the entire world will be blessed."

"A messiah?" Brooke sucked her mouth into a rosette. "You mean Jesus?"

Ethan felt himself stiffen. "Nay," he said softly, not wanting to upset her and cause trouble. "I doubt you would understand."

"Well, what do you have to do to be a Jew?" Brooke pressed, leaning forward. She seemed sincerely interested, and after studying her for a moment, Ethan decided that it wouldn't hurt to try and explain a little. It would be nice if someone aboard ship understood him.

"A Jew keeps the Law," he said, resting his hands upon his knees. "We honor God. We keep the Sabbath and the ancient festivals. We love mercy and try to walk humbly with God."

Brooke's face fell in disappointment. "That's all?"

"Isn't that enough?"

"It seems to be nothing special." Her fine, silky eyebrows rose a trifle. "You've been here with us all this time, and save for the fact that you pray a lot, I haven't noticed that you're much different from the rest of us. Kimberly prays a lot, too, and tells Bible stories—"

"I haven't been—" Ethan paused while the memory of his dream edged his teeth. For a moment he saw his father's fiery eyes superimposed on the rough planks of the wood. Those eyes had warned him—he must live as a Jew.

Ethan swallowed hard. "I haven't been living as I ought to. I thought that because I was not yet a man and because I was on this ship, God would understand if I didn't keep the Sabbath. But I think now I ought to follow the Law. My father would want me to. Even though I'm alone, I still need to keep the Sabbath and the holy days. It won't be easy, but 'tis what my father would want me to do."

Brooke looked at him with confusion in her eyes, then she managed a sweet smile that made Ethan's heart turn over. "I don't know of certain what you're talking about," she whispered, placing her cool hand on his. "But I know you'll do the right thing, Ethan Reis."

She stood up and walked away, but the space she had occupied seemed to vibrate softly as if she had changed it somehow. Ethan took a quick breath and looked back at the wall, then slowly began to sing his morning prayers.

119

16

Kimberly shifted uneasily before the captain. He sat at his desk, glaring up at her from his maps, and for a moment she wished Squeege hadn't bothered to ask Captain Blade if she might talk to him.

"Excuse me, sir," she began, pulling a stray strand of hair from her eyes, "but we have need of a few sheets of parchment. You see, none of us has a Bible, and though you have a prayer book, still, I thought it might be better if we had our own copy of the holy Scriptures. And since we have memorized sections of it, we thought we might write it out for ourselves."

"Y'are planning to write the Bible?" Captain Blade asked. His dark eyes danced with merriment even though he took pains to keep his face composed in stern lines. "Come, child, surely you can't be imagining that the Holy Spirit will speak through you."

"Nay, not at all," Kimberly said, twisting her hands.

"We don't want to write the Word of God according to our own wishes, but according to the memory of it in our minds. If you will be so good as to give us several sheets of parchment—"

"For such a foolish notion I can give you nothing," Captain Blade said, returning his attention to his maps. "Go back below, girl."

Kimberly stood her ground. "Please, sir," she said, begging. "You have no idea how difficult it is to keep order down below. I'm trying to do what my blessed mother wanted me to by helping the young ones, but with nothing to do and no standards to guide us, 'tis an awful burden. But if we had a bit of parchment, we'd have a task and the blessed Word of God to guide us. Surely you wouldn't be denying us that—"

Captain Blade sighed in exasperation and held up a hand. "Hush, girl, I've heard enough. I've not got parchment to spare, but I'll give you a single sheet if 'twill keep you quiet and out of my cabin."

"And a pen and ink?" Kimberly asked hopefully.

The captain shook his head in regret, but opened his desk drawer. "Here," he said, pulling a sheet of parchment from the desk. He slid the paper across the desk toward Kimberly, then pulled a small vial of ink and a quill pen from another drawer. "Use the ink sparingly, mind you, for there is no more to be had out here on the sea. And keep the brats below occupied, for we have work to do up here on the deck—"

A sudden call from the lookout outside interrupted the captain's words. "Captain Blade! Beggin' your pardon, sir, but you'd better come out here!"

Kimberly whirled as the captain swept by her, his face wary and dark. The parchment was wonderfully dry and crinkly in her hand, and she leaned over to pick up the vial of ink and the pen before the captain could change his mind.

122

She slipped out of the captain's cabin and was about to descend with her treasures, but a curious sight stopped her in her tracks. Squeege, Captain Blade, and a host of other seamen were gathered in a knot at the bow. Each man stared into the distance, and Kimberly followed the direction of their gaze and gasped at what she saw brooding on the face of the western sea.

Upon the waters, like an enormous forbidding hand, a gray cloud hovered. It was so dense that nothing could be seen within it and so broad that Kimberly could see neither its beginning nor end. The fog bank was tall enough to cloak a ship entirely and so cold that even from this distance she could feel its moist breath.

"Shall we go around, Captain?" Squeege was asking, his eyes narrowing in concern. "We know not what might be inside. Some say such cloud banks cover islands with coasts so rocky they'll cut a ship to shreds—"

"'Tis nothing but insubstantial fog, and 'twill bring us no harm to sail through it," another man interrupted. "When the sun rises higher, the cloud will burn off in a flash, leaving us a path of bright blue sea."

"What sun?" another sailor argued. "The clouds overhead are as heavy as the ones in the fog—"

"You cannot see in a fog," Squeege retorted. "How are we supposed to navigate if we can't see a foot in front of the ship? Ye have forgotten that one of the brats pitched the captain's compass overboard long ago."

123

"Fog can't last forever—"

"If our provisions are to last, we need to make good time, and that means sailing straight on through whatever lies ahead—"

"You cannot sail—"

"We must sail!"

"'Tis folly!"

"'Tis only fitting—"

"Be silent!" Captain Blade commanded. His furious

voice, lifted in a shout, stopped the babble of the seamen. Kimberly had a feeling that the captain would not want her on deck during this tense time, but she could not move, so great was her fascination with the huge gray cloud that hovered over the water. The seamen huddled on the deck around their captain; no one noticed her.

Captain Blade brushed back a dark tendril of hair that the wind had blown out of place. All the while he kept his eyes fastened to the gray mass. He seemed to be weighing the risks of changing course to sail around the cloud versus sailing through it. While he thought, his men waited, rubbing their hands on their arms and glancing anxiously at the stone-colored mountain of fog that rode the sea.

"'Tis the Sargasso Sea," the captain finally said, his face empty of all expression. "'Tis noted for its deadly calms and fields of seaweed. Look there, in the water, and ye will see."

As one, Kimberly and the crew peered over the edge of the ship's railing. Heavy mats of dark greenish-brown seaweed filled the waters and brushed up against the sides of the ship with each lap of the waves.

"Christopher Columbus entered these waters in 1492," the captain continued, "and recorded observations of an unexplained white glowing in the sea. I wonder"— Captain Blade scratched his beard as his eyes raked the gray form in front of his ship—"I wonder if he saw a sight to equal this one."

"I've heard tales of the Sargasso Sea," one of the seamen spoke up, his eyes rolling in fright. "They say that if a ship is becalmed here, she'll grow grass and barnacles till she's unable to sail. Then borer worms will begin to eat their way into the vessel till she's a rotted and putrid mess, manned only by skeletons, a ghost ship—"

"Enough," Captain Blade barked, silencing the man

with a harsh glance. "Mister Squeege, what think you of the wind?"

Squeege shrugged. "'Tis hard to say with any certainty, Captain. We've a fair breeze out here, but what will blow in the cloud, I cannot say."

"Mister Jones," the captain called up to the lookout entwined in the rigging. "What think you of the size of the cloud?"

The man at the top of the mainmast covered his eyes with his hand and stared off toward the horizon. "I can't see an end to it, Captain," he finally answered, his voice ringing over the deck. "The monster has a clean edge, so we could sail northward around it, but there's no guaranteeing that it won't move in the night to cover us no matter where we go."

"Then we'll continue straight ahead," Captain Blade called, his voice ringing with authority. "Mister Squeege, raise the foresail and mainsails only; leave off topsails for now. We'll go slowly through, not at any great pace, and I want lookouts at the port and starboard bow in addition to Mister Jones on the mainmast."

"Aye, sir," Squeege called. The knot of huddled men broke up as each man returned to his post, and Kimberly flinched when Squeege's round eyes fell upon her.

"What are you still doing up here?" he demanded.

"I'm going now," she answered, lifting the hatch to the companionway.

"Wait, missy." Squeege's hand fell upon her arm. "Not a word of what you've heard here to the others, do you understand? I don't want a load of frightened young'uns below."

"Not a word," Kimberly answered, taking a deep breath. She didn't completely understand the strange situation herself, and she didn't want to frighten the others.

She slipped into the dim light of the passageway, then paused to listen to the hubbub on deck. Captain

Blade's crew were seasoned sailors, and she knew there was very little that could surprise them. But from their strained faces and jerky movements she could tell that the cold stillness of the fog bank and the stories of the Sargasso Sea had disturbed them greatly. Goose bumps lifted on her legs as she crept back down to the hold.

* * *

While the other children squealed with delight as the *Seven Brothers* sailed into the cloud, Ethan felt a thin, cold blade of foreboding slice into his heart. The ship moved slowly and surely into the mist, and it was suddenly as if time and space ceased to exist. The wide expanse of blue ocean disappeared, and a chilly, pearl-colored mist spilled from the windows into the children's hold. The sails overhead ceased to snap in the wind, and the soft mist covered the ship like a blanket.

"'Tis like a fairyland," Brooke trilled from her place at the window, but Ethan could see nothing magical or charming about the cushioning silence of the fog. It was a bleak emptiness, a gray film that had come to cover him in confusion. The ship had entered a vast stretch of nothingness, and Ethan felt the same emptiness inside his soul.

126 Kimberly Hollis stood near him, her much-sought-after parchment and ink in her hands. But even she seemed distracted when the ship entered the fog bank. She was studying the wide windows with a worried, frightened expression on her face. When she felt Ethan's eyes upon her, she raised her eyes to his in an oddly keen, swift look. It was then Ethan realized that she felt the same dread he did.

* * *

Kimberly shook off her vague apprehensions not long after the ship entered the fog bank. The Sargasso Sea was nothing to worry about; hadn't Columbus sailed through it with no trouble? "'Tis nothing but fog, and the seamen

say 'twill burn off as soon as the sun gets hot," she told
the younger ones who had gathered around her with their
questions. "Sailors see such things every day, after all. 'Tis
nothing to worry about. Besides, I have something much
more important for us to consider. We need a copy of the
holy Scriptures, and since none of us has a Bible at hand,
we shall try to write what we can from memory."

"The entire Bible?" Brooke said, crinkling her nose.

"Nay," Kimberly answered, nodding primly. "Only
as much as we can fit on one sheet of parchment. Captain
Blade was most—" She paused. She wanted to say *stingy*,
but it wouldn't have been nice to describe the captain
with such a word. "The captain was very *careful* lest we
deplete his store of supplies, so we only have one sheet. I
think we should write Old Testament verses on one side
of the paper, and New Testament verses on the other.
And we need someone to be our scribe, someone who can
write neatly and in a very small script."

"I can write very well," Brooke said, lifting her hand.
The others snorted in disbelief, and the girl's cheeks
flamed. "Well, I can! My tutors have always praised my
penmanship."

"Then you shall write our Scriptures," Kimberly
said, feeling generous. She passed the parchment, pen,
and ink to Brooke, who spread them out on the floor.
Kimberly crossed her legs and rested her hands on her
knees. "Now, who can begin by telling us a Bible verse?
Does anyone know the first verse in the Bible?"

The younger children twittered among themselves,
but no one ventured to speak. Kimberly rolled her eyes
and looked toward Thatcher with a questioning glance.
He shook his head. Kimberly then turned to Wingate,
who only ran his hands through his hair and shrugged.

"Does anyone know the first verse of the Bible?"
Kimberly asked again, amazed that no one would answer.

Ethan's voice broke the stillness. "'In the beginning

God created the heaven and the earth,'" he said, his voice resonating through the hold. He spoke slowly, as though he were feeling his way, and Kimberly snapped her fingers at Brooke so the other girl would begin to write.

"'And the earth was without form, and void; and darkness was upon the face of the deep,'" Ethan continued. "'And the Spirit of God moved upon the face of the waters. And God said, Let there be light: and there was light.'"

"Slow down," Brooke called, dipping her quill pen into the bottle of ink. She pressed her lips together and continued to write, ". . . created . . . the . . . heaven . . . and . . . earth." She looked up triumphantly. "What's next?"

Ethan frowned. "This is a bad idea. I won't do it."

"Nay, don't stop!" Kimberly cried, leaning toward him in her eagerness. "You were doing so well. Please— how much can you say?"

Ethan looked away toward the shadowy mist outside the windows. "I know all of the Scriptures—the Torah, Joshua, Judges, Samuel, Kings, Isaiah, Jeremiah, Ezekiel, the Twelve Prophets, Psalms, Proverbs, Job, Canticles, Ruth, Lamentations, Ecclesiastes, Esther, Daniel, Ezra-Nehemiah, and Chronicles. I have known them since I was a boy."

128

"That's wonderful," Kimberly said, clapping her hands in joy. "Why, you can dictate the entire Old Testament to us!"

"Nay," Ethan said, turning his head further away. "I do not wish to have any part of this."

Baffled, Kimberly looked at Brooke with a question in her eyes, but the other girl only shrugged. Why would Ethan suddenly decide not to help? Had Brooke been too slow with the pen? Or was he somehow offended because Kimberly had mentioned including the New Testament on her sheet of parchment?

She decided not to press Ethan. His strange and disagreeable mood would pass. "Why don't we think about the rest of the Scriptures?" she said, turning to the others. "What verses do you know?"

Wingate stood to his feet and removed his cap from his head. Speaking slowly and very distinctly, he began to recite: "'And it came to pass in those days, that there went out a decree from Caesar Augustus, that all the world should be taxed. And all went to be taxed, every one into his own city. And Joseph also went up from Galilee, out of the city of Nazareth, into Judaea, unto the city of David, which is called Bethlehem; (because he was of the house and lineage of David:) To be taxed with Mary his espoused wife, being great with child.'"

White fog from the cloud swirled around Wingate's feet, providing a soft backdrop to his speech. "'And so it was, that, while they were there, the days were accomplished that she should be delivered. And she brought forth her firstborn son, and wrapped him in swaddling clothes, and laid him in a manger; because there was no room for them in the inn. And there were in the same country shepherds abiding in the field, keeping watch over their flock by night. And, lo, the angel of the Lord came upon them, and the glory of the Lord shone round about them: and they were sore afraid. And the angel said unto them, Fear not: for, behold, I bring you good tidings of great joy, which shall be to all people. For unto you is born this day in the city of David a Saviour, which is Christ the Lord. And this shall be a sign unto you; Ye shall find the babe wrapped in swaddling clothes, lying in a manger. And suddenly there was with the angel a multitude of the heavenly host praising God, and saying, Glory to God in the highest, and on earth peace, good will toward men.'"

129

Wingate finished with a flourish of his cap and a bow. Kimberly and the others applauded and cheered.

"Of course, you'll have to repeat all of that," Brooke said, laughing as she clapped. "You spoke too quickly for me to get it all down."

"How'd you learn all that?" Thatcher called. "I thought you said you didn't know any holy writ."

"When my mother was alive," Wingate said, sitting cross-legged on the floor, "the master and mistress of the house always had the servants play the parts of Mary and Joseph at Christmas. I was enjoined to learn that Scripture and tell the story each year. My mother was Mary— that is, until she died." His voice clotted with emotion and for a moment he looked at the floor, unable to go on.

Kimberly felt a lump rise in her own throat, so she was grateful when Brooke kept the conversation going. "Well, come over here and repeat the Scripture again," Brooke said, uncorking the ink bottle. "But slowly, this time."

* * *

Ethan stirred uneasily in his sleep as his dream visitor came to him again. "You wander in the mists of confusion, my son," his father said in a husky night voice. His eyes were like a stream of gold in the dark, chasing the shadows away. "These vapors of chaos and unrest will not leave until you assume your rightful place in this world. You are a Jew, a son of Abraham and Jacob. Remember the sayings of the prophets and live according to the words of the Torah."

Suddenly a chorus of voices filled Ethan's dream: flat voices, harsh voices, nasal voices, hooting voices, rumbling voices, whispering voices. They spoke of the Torah, they quoted words from the prophets of old who had spoken with God:

"I will bless them that bless thee, and curse him that curseth thee: and in thee shall all families of the earth be blessed."

130

"Hear, O Israel: The Lord our God is one Lord."

"Thou mightest fear the Lord thy God, to keep all his statutes and his commandments, which I command thee, thou, and thy son, and thy son's son, all the days of thy life."

"The kings of the earth set themselves, and the rulers take counsel together, against the Lord, and against his anointed, saying—"

"Behold my servant, whom I uphold—"

"For he shall grow up before him as a tender plant, and as a root out of a dry ground—"

"—mine elect, in whom my soul delighteth; I have put my spirit upon him: he shall bring forth judgment to the Gentiles."

"—But thou, Bethlehem Ephratah, though thou be little among the thousands of Judah, yet out of thee shall he come forth unto me that is to be ruler in Israel, whose goings forth have been from of old, from everlasting—"

A clear, young voice rose over the others. "And Joseph also went up from Galilee, out of the city of Nazareth, into Judaea, unto the city of David, which is called Bethlehem. . . . And so it was, that, while they were there, the days were accomplished that she should be delivered."

This was Wingate's voice, and he was speaking of the baby born to Mary and Joseph.

"Nay!" Ethan sat up in a cold sweat, shivering.

17

I'm telling you, Captain, there's certain to be a remora holding the ship!"

Squeege's loud voice boomed from above and woke Kimberly from a vague half-sleep. She sat up, blinking in the dull gray light of the fog, and tuned her ears to the conversation drifting down from the upper deck.

"A remora!" Captain Blade retorted sharply. "They are native to the eastern seas, not these waters. And how could any fish live in the mats of seaweed below?"

"If 'tis all the same to you, sir, me and the men would like to have a look below. We'll put a couple o' men in the water to scrape off anything that might be holding us back—"

"'Tis too dangerous. What if ye become tangled in those weeds? I'll not be losing my crew here."

"If you please, sir, the men are growing a mite desperate. It might be fitting to give them something to do—a task, as it were. We'll tie stout ropes around their bellies and pull 'em up regular if you like."

Silence followed for a moment, then the captain grumbled his assent. "I still say 'tis folly to imagine that a remora is holding us in this place," he said. "An eight-inch sucker fish has no power over such a ship as this!"

* * *

Sitting alone by the window, Ethan lowered his head into his hands and kneaded his forehead. His head ached from memories of the dreams he'd been having for the last two nights. Visions of his father haunted his sleep, and in the morning Ethan awoke confused and sad. He *wanted* to be a good Jew. He *wanted* to obey God. But how could such a thing be done on a ship full of Gentiles in the middle of nowhere?

For that was where Ethan felt the *Seven Brothers* had gone—nowhere. For twenty-four hours the ship had ridden a sea that did not move. Day and night were nearly alike in the fog. The brightness of the sun was barely visible through the thick mist that had engulfed the vessel, and the moon lit it with a dim luminescent glow. The fog was a ghostly vapor that wove itself in and out of every nook and cranny of the ship, and Ethan knew even the bravest of the children were beginning to feel a little spooked by the eerie silence of the sea and the choking cloud that had surrounded them.

As he sat alone, Ethan grappled with a disturbing thought. Was his dream a prophecy? His father had said that Ethan would remain lost until he assumed his place in the world. But how could he *find* his place as long as he was lost in a fog? It was a no-win situation, a puzzle without an answer, a riddle that made no sense. Ethan had always prided himself on his intellect and the ease with which he learned, but he could find no solutions to his problem aboard the *Seven Brothers*. Though he had committed pages and pages of the Hebrew Bible and the

Talmud to memory, no answers sprang from its pages to confront the questions in his mind.

If a Jew prays alone, does God hear him? he quizzed himself. *The Mishna says that ten Jewish males are necessary to form a synagogue so that prayers can be said, so how can I pray alone? If I pray and observe the Sabbath, will my efforts mean anything if no one prays with me? If a tree falls in the forest, does it make a sound if no one is there to hear it?*

His doubt and guilt grew when he considered the possibility that the ship had been becalmed in a cloud because of his failure to obey the Law. He remembered the story of Jonah and the great fish. God had sent a great storm to afflict a ship much like this one because the rebellious Jonah was aboard. Only after the seamen cast Jonah into the ocean were the seas calmed again. Should he tell Captain Blade of his disobedience and offer to jump overboard? Or mayhap he should just throw himself over the ship's railing and let the others sail on to Virginia without ever knowing of his disgrace.

If I do nothing—Ethan raised his eyes to the sea and gazed out upon the swirling mist—*every soul aboard will starve, for we will eventually use up the provisions Captain Blade recently acquired. No one will reach Virginia if this monstrous fog does not soon lift.*

135

* * *

"Hallo!"

The grinning, toothless sailor called greetings to the captives as he was lowered past their open window into the water. Stripped of his shirt, the sailor wore only his breeches and the rope that tied him to a secure yardarm. A gleaming knife was tucked into the fabric at his waist.

"What is he looking for?" Wingate asked Ethan.

Ethan frowned. "I know not. Barnacles or weeds, I suppose. Sailors are a superstitious lot. They place their trust in rituals, not in the Master of the universe."

"'Twould seem to me a good idea to place one's trust in a strong and sturdy rope," Wingate said as the cord holding the seaman creaked and groaned. He turned to Ethan and grinned. "And in God, too, of course. I don't suppose a strong rope will do much good when we stand before our Maker, eh?"

"Nay," Ethan answered, abruptly turning his attention back to the water, where the sailor dove underwater to search for anything that might be holding the ship. It was a useless effort, Ethan knew. *He* was the reason for this trouble.

* * *

In the dim light of the lower hold, Kimberly frowned as she watched Ethan nibble on his hardtack without enthusiasm. He had not been himself lately, and she wondered if she had offended him. At the beginning of the voyage, Ethan had been kind and considerate toward her, even sympathetic when her mother died. Since then, he had been a voice of reason and help. But in the last few days he carried a weight of sadness on his thin face. He sat alone by the window and refused all who tried to talk to him.

136 *What happened?* Kimberly wondered, thinking back over the events of the last week. *He seems so worried, but I thought Ethan was one of the strongest of us.*

When the captives had returned to their hold, Kimberly moved toward Ethan and sat down beside him. "Now, Ethan," she said, covering his hand with hers even as he tried to pull away, "I know you're upset about something. But I want to be your friend. And no matter how you try to hide it, I want to know the truth. I'm not leaving your side until the entire story's been told, so begin at the beginning and tell me what has made you so downhearted."

Ethan's face emptied of expression and locked. As

she waited, Kimberly thought that he would not speak at all, for an icy silence fell between them.

"Please, Ethan," she whispered, lowering her voice. "I won't tell the others if you do not want me to. I care about you, and I want to know what's troubling you."

He grimaced as though she'd hurt him. "You cannot understand," he whispered.

"Mayhap I cannot," she answered, leaning closer. "But I can listen."

The harsh lines of Ethan's face suddenly relaxed, and a torrent of words began to flow. Kimberly was stunned by the sound of tears in Ethan's voice. He spoke of his dreams and of his father's warning about not living as a Jew. "You don't know, Kimberly, you can't understand," he said again, his face distorted with feeling. "I was part of a family and now I am totally alone—"

"We have all lost our families," Kimberly quietly pointed out. "You're not alone in this, Ethan."

"But mine was a Jewish family," Ethan answered, swiping his hand through his curly hair. "My family was one in a chain of families, and now I am utterly cut off from them. A Jew's duty is to worship in a synagogue of ten men, a *minyan*, and I am only one! How am I to worship anywhere? And I do not dare neglect my obligation. My father warned me—"

"You're not yet a man," Kimberly said, trying to soothe him. "Mayhap God will send the other nine men you need by the time you are grown."

"A Jew is a man when he is thirteen," Ethan answered, lifting his shoulders in unconscious pride. "In two years I will be a man. If I were with my family I would have a bar mitzvah and be called up to read the Torah in the synagogue. I would wear my prayer shawl, and when I had done reading in Hebrew, the others would wish me *chazak baruch*—"

"Which is?" Kimberly asked.

137

"Be strong and blessed," Ethan answered, resting his chin on his folded arms as he stared into the unearthly mist beyond the window. "How can I be strong when I am alone? Solomon, the wisest man who ever lived—"

"I know about Solomon," Kimberly interrupted. "He's in our Bible, too. He wrote Proverbs, Canticles, and Ecclesiastes."

Ethan lifted an eyebrow in surprise. "If you know him, then you must know that he wrote 'Two are better than one; because they have a good reward for their labour. For if they fall, the one will lift up his fellow: but woe to him that is alone when he falleth; for he hath not another to help him up.'"

"That is a good verse to write on our parchment," Kimberly answered, making a mental note to remind Brooke of it. "But truly, you're not alone, Ethan." She reached out to touch his arm. "You have us. We're not Jewish, but we care for you. We'll support you and pray with you if you want us to. And God is always with you—"

"I can't feel him," Ethan cried, jerking away from her grasp. "I felt him in the synagogue, in the prayers of my father, and in the candles at our Sabbath table. I don't have any of that here, Kimberly. And I don't think God is here, either, no matter how much you pray to him!"

Kimberly pressed her lips together, stunned by his outburst, and Ethan's eyes clouded. "Now go away, please," he said, regaining control of his temper. "Just leave me alone. You don't understand. You couldn't. You aren't Jewish."

* * *

After Kimberly stumbled away, hurt and silent, Ethan sat under an avalanche of guilt and blamed himself for his outburst. He was wrong, of course, to yell at her. She had only been trying to help, and it wasn't her fault that he had been separated from his parents and put on this ship.

It wasn't even her fault that he was a poor excuse for a Jewish boy and that he had failed his father. Nothing was Kimberly's fault, and yet he had yelled at her.

The creeping fog outside was beginning to lose some of its brightness, and Ethan guessed the sun was setting somewhere beyond the wall of mist. Today, by his reckoning, was Friday, and when the sun set it would be the Sabbath. He was not to work, not to sew, not to do anything but rest and think about family and the things of God. But it hurt too much to think about his family, so if he were to find any salvation at all, he would have to spend the next twenty-four hours thinking about God.

Mayhap this is what God wants, he told himself. *If I can keep the Sabbath, God will see that I can be a good Jew away from home. My father will rest in peace knowing that I am keeping the Sabbath where I am, and our hearts will be joined across the miles. God will smile and release the ship from this cloud of judgment, and I will be free.*

"How long, O Lord, will you ignore our cries?" he whispered, echoing the words his father had often murmured as he prayed for deliverance and the coming of the Messiah. "How long must we wait?"

He would soon discover how long. If he was perfect and kept the Law, maybe the Almighty would release the ship. Ethan resolved to be a perfect Jew on the morrow and stretched out on the floor to sleep. He had no sooner closed his eyes, though, than someone nudged him with the wooden sole of a shoe.

139

"Ethan Reis, I used to think you were a bright lad, but now I know you're a foolish dolt!"

He squinted with one eye and looked up. Kimberly Hollis stood above him, her hands on her hips, her eyes flaming. He gave her a slow, reluctant smile. "I think you're right," he said, sitting up. "I was wrong to speak so harshly to you, and I hope you will forgive me."

The anger left her eyes, and Kimberly's mouth

twisted in a half smile. "I may." She lowered her hands and sat next to him on the floor. "I couldn't believe that you'd be so rude as to turn down an offer of help."

"I need help, but not the kind you're offering," Ethan said, crossing his legs and pulling his knees to him. "Tomorrow is the Sabbath, Kimberly, and I can't do any work."

She snorted. "Who works on this ship? I'm doing well if I can get the younger ones to pay attention for the space of an hour whilst I'm trying to teach them."

"I can't fetch anything," Ethan said, patiently explaining. "For instance, I won't be able to go down into the hold and eat dinner, for I'd have to carry it from one place to another. So, if you're still willing to help me, I'd appreciate it if you'd bring me my dinner tomorrow. I'll have to eat something, for this Sunday is a fast day when all Jews must not eat anything."

"So many rules!" Kimberly said, looking at him with a doubtful expression in her eyes. "Eat and don't eat. Walk, but don't carry anything. Who invented all these dos and don'ts?"

Ethan shook his head. "You wouldn't understand. They are ancient laws that have come down from holy rabbis. If you want to help me, that's what I need. If you don't want to help, well—'tis your choice."

Kimberly looked at him as if she were weighing her decision, then she slowly nodded. "I'll do what I can to help you, Ethan," she said. "But I don't think eating or not eating is going to solve your problem."

"'Twill show God that I'm trying to keep the Law," Ethan said. "And mayhap 'twill save the ship. If God is pleased with me, he will lead us out of this fog."

"I don't know," Kimberly said, giving him a look that was both compassionate and troubled. "Who can say what the morrow will bring?"

Saturday, June 5

18

Kimberly smoothed the single sheet of parchment upon the floor and gazed at what hours of work had produced: the most garbled, mixed up, hodgepodge collection of Scripture verses she had ever seen. Brooke's handwriting, which was neat and tiny at the top of the page, grew more loose and large with each succeeding verse. There was very little empty space left upon the New Testament page. Wingate's version of the birth of Christ was there, in glowing detail, and so were verses about the many mansions in heaven, Jesus being the Light of the World, and "For God so loved the world, that he gave his only begotten Son, that whosoever believeth in him should not perish, but have everlasting life."

The Old Testament page was in far worse shape. Thatcher had but one verse to contribute to the entire project, and Kimberly had grimaced when he offered his quote: "Now it came to pass."

"That's it?" she said, disappointment heavy in her voice.

"'Tis a great verse," he said, punctuating the air with his finger. "My mother used to say it, God rest her soul. Whenever I'd get into trouble, she'd say, 'Thank God, the Bible tells me this has come to pass.'"

"'Tis a silly verse for us to write down," Kimberly protested, thinking of the precious space the verse would take on her only sheet of parchment.

"I like it," Abigail said, coming to Thatcher's defense. The others were so unused to hearing Abigail speak that they grew quiet and agreed that "now it came to pass" was worthy to be included in their collection of Scripture.

After that, the children's memories grew more and more disorganized. Kimberly knew that Ethan could help them a great deal if he would, but he sat quietly by himself, determined to observe the Sabbath. At dinnertime Kimberly brought him his hardtack and cup of water, and he did not move from his spot, but took the food from her with only a smile of thanks. It was almost as if he was afraid to break his silence, and though Kimberly didn't think *talking* was forbidden on the Sabbath, she didn't think Ethan was taking any chances. He dedicated the entire day to God.

After sundown, when the Sabbath was officially over, Ethan crept over to where she lay and whispered his thanks. "I did it," he said, his eyes glowing in confidence. "I kept the Law as perfectly as I knew how. I didn't work. I didn't talk. I didn't do anything that would dishonor God."

"And do you think God was pleased?" Kimberly asked.

"We'll see on the morrow," Ethan answered, his eyes shining like beacons of light in the gathering darkness. "I wouldn't be at all surprised if the wind blew the clouds of mist away tonight. And now I know I shall sleep easily and without dreams of my father. He will be pleased because I have done well."

"I'm glad that's finished," Kimberly murmured, resting her cheek on her hand. "I'm ready to see more of the old Ethan."

"'Tis not finished," Ethan said. "Every Sabbath I must do the same thing. And the morrow is the twenty-second day of the Jewish month called Sivan. I must fast in memory of Jeroboam."

"What?" Kimberly sat up, more awake now. "You must do what?"

"I cannot eat," Ethan said, shrugging. "Jeroboam was a wicked king who forbade his people to worship God in Jerusalem. So we fast and think about his wickedness so we will not follow his example."

"You have to eat," Kimberly said, lowering her voice. She raised her eyes to look carefully at her friend. Behind his young face, a worried, intense old man peered out from his eyes. "Ethan, none of us has had a decent meal since we left London. We're barely getting enough food to keep from starving. We're naught but skin and bones, so 'tis foolish to fast."

Ethan set his jaw. "I must fast," he said, crossing his arms. "And I will. I will show God that I am determined to be a good Jew."

"You'll starve faster than the rest of us, then," Kimberly said, slamming her hand down upon the floor in frustration. Ethan's eyes held hers for a long moment, then he stood and walked away. Kimberly waited until he had gone, then she rubbed her throbbing hand. She had slammed it down with quite a bit of force, but she would not let Ethan know how badly it hurt.

"Dear heavenly Father," she prayed as she flexed her hand. "Help me know how to reach Ethan. He wants to please you, but he is so caught up in *doing* things that I

143

don't know how to reach his heart. He is one of your chosen people, God, so please pull him toward you."

* * *

Ethan's bones grated on the hard planking beneath him as he tossed and turned, unable to sleep. How dare Kimberly tell him not to fast! She seemed to be religious, she prayed all the time, and yet she didn't want him to do the things that he knew were his religious duty. For all her talk about God and the Bible, she didn't understand anything he was trying to do. He was striving to be holy and spiritual and godly. Couldn't she see that?

He rolled onto his stomach and propped his head upon his folded arms. All around him children slept, their breaths rattling in the humid night air as the chill mist floated through the hold and over the ship. It was a ghostly scene, and Ethan scrunched his eyes together and automatically began to recite the words to a psalm he repeated whenever he was afraid: "The Lord is my light and my salvation; whom shall I fear? The Lord is the strength of my life; of whom shall I be afraid? . . . Though an host should encamp against me, my heart shall not fear: though war should rise against me, in this will I be confident."

144

His conscience suddenly struck him: Was he using those words like a charm to keep evil away, or did he truly believe them? If he believed them, why did the gray clamminess of the mist frighten him beyond reason? He was a good Jew. He tried his best to keep the Law. Even if the Master of the universe took him down into the depths of the ocean, he had no reason to fear.

Yet he was afraid. And Kimberly Hollis faced the fog with more confidence than he did. He had seen her nervous, upset, and angry, but in times of true trouble and danger, she had always worn a look of peace. When Mistress Hollis had died, Kimberly wiped her mother's face with a tear-streaked hand, and yet she had not felt hopeless. And while it was obvious that the fog concerned her, Kimberly thought more about collecting her precious snippets of Scripture than fretting over the unknown.

Was being a Christian so simple? It would be easy to announce to the others that he had decided to follow the Christ. They would be glad and life would be easy, for he would no longer be different. He could forget his Hebrew, disregard the Talmud, live freely on the Sabbath, and not worry about the rules and regulations of his own religious life.

But it wouldn't be *real*. Anything accepted blindly, without thought or testing, was accepted foolishly. And being Jewish was too much a part of Ethan's life to be put away like a pair of outgrown shoes.

For the flash of an instant, Ethan envied Kimberly for her confidence in her religious beliefs. She did not worry about duty; she just *lived*. She prayed because she wanted to. She sang songs from her heart. She cared and worked with and for the others because she was honestly concerned for them. And when she was wrong, Kimberly apologized, recognized her failing, and set about making things right. She did nothing out of duty; she acted and reacted out of love.

Love for whom? Ethan wondered. Her mother was dead. Her father was waiting in Virginia, and Kimberly had often said that she had only a vague memory of him. So who was Kimberly Hollis trying to impress with her good deeds? God perhaps. But God didn't want goodness. He wanted sacrifices and obedience and honor. He demanded perfection.

"So be it. I've been perfect, God," Ethan muttered, knowing that God probably wasn't listening, because Ethan wasn't in a congregation of ten men. But if the Master of the universe was truly all-powerful, he certainly could hear. Maybe he'd listen. "If you, Master of the

145

universe, could take us out of this cloud," Ethan went on, "I'll know that you've seen me and that you are pleased."

He waited for a moment and heard nothing. Then a muted cry from the deck lifted the hairs on his forearms. "Great Caesar's ghost!" one of the seamen yelled. "Saints preserve us! 'Tis Saint Elmo's fire!"

Desperately curious to know if God had already answered his prayer, Ethan sat up and crept quietly forward on his hands and knees. No one else in the hold stirred. Moving carefully through the sleeping bodies, he climbed up the narrow companionway and pushed open the hatch.

His mouth fell open in amazement at the strange sight that greeted him. The entire ship's crew crowded around the mainmast. All the seamen were staring upward, and several were openly weeping. High atop the mast sat a ball of flickering, bluish light.

"What a blessed sight," one sailor was saying, wiping tears from his cheeks without embarrassment. "I feared we were sailing off the edge of the world, but God has sent this sign to assure us that he's watchin' over us."

"Saint Elmo, the patron of mariners," Squeege announced, his broad face tilted toward the bluish light. "I don't know if it be a sign or a warning, but 'tis frightful strange, true enough."

146

"I heard those on Ferdinand Magellan's ship first saw the light a hundred years ago," another sailor volunteered. "They say the saint appears to a few as a good omen."

Ethan squinted upward toward the light. He didn't believe in saints, or in fairies, or in anything magical, but his heart yearned toward the light in the way a moth is drawn to a candle. Was this the sign God had sent him? Had he done well in his effort to please the Master of the universe? Or was this merely another freak phenomenon of nature, a cousin to the persistent and cursed fog?

The strange ball of light opened the door on memories of his father's stories. Moses had seen a burning bush that was not consumed by flames, just as the top of the mainmast did not dissolve in the heat of the flickering blue fire. And a pillar of fire had led the children of Israel through the wilderness on their journey from the bondage of Egypt to the freedom of the Promised Land. It would be like God to send a sign of fire, for he had done it ofttimes before.

"You know what this reminds me of?" one of the seamen called to Squeege. "The star of Bethlehem, do ye recall it? It came and stood over the place where the holy babe Jesus was born."

Jesus again. Ethan shook his head as if he could jolt the words from his ears. He crept back below as the sailors continued to stare at the curious apparition above the mainmast. The bizarre flickering blue ball of light danced across the back of Ethan's eyelids as he closed his eyes to sleep.

Sunday, June 6

19

Kimberly and the others overheard the seamen talking about the brief appearance of "Saint Elmo's fire" when they woke up the next morning. Even though the cloud had not lifted and the ship still sat in a thick soup of unwavering fog, the spirits of the seamen were considerably lighter since the arrival of what they considered a heavenly visitation.

"I don't care what they say, I don't think what they saw had anything to do with a saint," Kimberly insisted as she talked to Wingate and Thatcher. "If God wanted to tell us something, he'd *tell* us, not send some freakish light to dance around on top of the mainmast."

"What harm will it do to let them think whatever they like?" Thatcher said, shrugging. "You take the fun out of everything, Kimberly Hollis."

Kimberly turned her back on him and crossed her arms. Sometimes Thatcher could make her so angry! He was wrong, of course. She didn't enjoy taking the fun out of things. She just didn't believe in encouraging things that weren't true. She didn't tell the younger children, for instance, that they'd be adopted by wonderful people and live happily ever after in Virginia, because that wasn't likely to happen. She told them the honest facts about life in Jamestown as she knew it. She said they'd be sold into indentured service and were likely to find the work hard, the food rough, and the Indians hostile. But if they worked well, prayed diligently, and tried their best, they might actually thrive in the new colony. Her father had beaten the odds. And with the blessings of God, the others could, too.

So why should she encourage the sailors to believe they'd been visited by an angel or some sort of saint when it wasn't true? God didn't send heavenly visitors down without a purpose, and she couldn't find any purpose in the vision that had appeared last night. No one had been saved or spared from danger, and no voice had spoken from heaven to assure them that they were in God's will. It was foolishness to believe that such things were of God when there was sure to be a rational explanation.

She glanced over at Ethan. On any other day he would have been quick to supply a good explanation for the light, but today he sat alone again, his face turned toward the gray murk lingering outside the window. She remembered that today was a special fast day for the Jews, which meant Ethan wouldn't be eating. She felt a stab of sympathy for him. Though it was but midmorning, already she was so hungry she could have eaten her share of food and ten other plateful besides.

Mayhap, she thought, noticing that he was clutching his stomach, *I should be more forthright when I talk to him about Jesus. I've dropped hints and gentle suggestions, but I've never completely explained why Jesus has to be the Messiah he waits for.*

But Ethan was one of God's chosen people. Had she any right to meddle in his religion? After all, he was one of the most devout, sincere, and gentle boys she had ever met. If she had judged him by his actions and words alone, she would have thought him a Christian, for he was quick to help and always thoughtful in his consideration for others. Didn't he have the right to believe as he chose to? Maybe a loving God wouldn't judge Ethan too harshly, for he was honest and kind. . . .

Unbidden, a portion of Scripture sprang from her memory as clearly as if it had been written on the floor in front of her: *For I am not ashamed of the gospel of Christ: for it is the power of God unto salvation to every one that believeth; to the Jew first, and also to the Greek.*

"I am not ashamed," she whispered as the light of understanding dawned in her heart, "because Ethan needs the salvation of Christ just as I do. Whether Jew or Gentile, everyone needs the Savior."

Knowing this, she bowed her head and prayed that God would show her how to approach her friend.

* * *

Ethan clutched his belly as his stomach cramped again. He had done nothing but think about bread and meat and fruit since the sun rose, and tantalizing thoughts of the food he had resolved not to eat caused his stomach to rumble uncontrollably. He didn't know if he could fast. This was only midmorning, and yet he felt absolutely weak with hunger.

"For thou, O Lord, are the bread of life," he murmured, remembering a phrase his father had often quoted. "You fed us with manna in the wilderness; now feed my soul with the bread of heaven."

Food. His stomach tightened, and his palms began to sweat as his mouth watered. How on earth could he ever make it through the day without eating? He had the

151

healthy appetite of a growing boy. And Kimberly was right, he hadn't eaten enough in the last few weeks. Even now his breeches hung loosely about his waist, and his legs were as thin as reeds.

He tried to concentrate on wicked Jeroboam, but instead he thought of the fish and breads his mother used to bake for the family's Sabbath meals. He closed his eyes to picture Israel's wicked king and saw visions of heaping bowls of vegetables and fruits on his family's dinner table.

The fog still covered the ship like a dense blanket, so God was still testing him. The Master of the universe waited to see how perfect and devout Ethan Reis could be.

Was it fair of God to hold everyone in the calm? Captain Blade was worried about being stranded in the calm. Ethan could hear the fear in his voice. The seamen were either in a panic or a state of bliss due to the bizarre goings-on of the night before. And as long as the ship remained in the thick fog, the captain could not navigate. Every star, the moon, and even the sun itself was obscured by the leaden cloud bank.

The situation was entirely his fault. *I want to be a good Jew*, Ethan thought, clenching his fists. That thought ran through his mind as steadily as the lap of the waves even as, later in the day, he stood with the others and descended into the lower hold for dinner.

I want to be a good Jew, and I don't want to eat. He gritted his teeth as he put his hand out for the plate of hardtack and a slab of dried beef.

I want to be a good Jew and keep the fast. The words buzzed in his brain even as his mouth opened and he chewed the dry, tasteless sea biscuit.

When the meal was done and he had broken his promise to God and himself, Ethan climbed back up the companionway and sat at his place, silent and sullen.

He had failed.

Everything in him wanted to be a good Jew, a

152

perfect son of Abraham. Yet he couldn't do something as simple as fasting for one day.

He lowered his head to his knees and wept silently.

* * *

From across the hold, Kimberly lifted her head from her knees and saw that Ethan's thin shoulders were shaking. *He's crying!* she thought, then she remembered his determination to fast. She had seen him eating and thought nothing of it. But apparently Ethan considered his surrender to temptation a very great defeat.

She shifted her weight, intending to go talk to him, but a quiet inner voice urged her to stay still. One of the verses on the parchment leapfrogged into her thoughts: *Be still, and know that I am God.*

"Be still," she murmured, resting her cheek on her knees again. Outside the wide window, milky streaks of white shone through the haunted waters of the strange Sargasso Sea. Not a breeze moved over the waters; not a single breath of fresh air stirred to move the sticky, heavy cloud from the *Seven Brothers.*

"The entire ship is still, Lord," she whispered. "What do you want to show us?"

Be still. There were no other answers in the swirl of ghostly fog.

153

Monday, June 7

20

Kimberly and the others gaped in surprise when Captain Blade entered their hold before dinner on Monday afternoon. She cast a quick glance at Thatcher and Brooke that asked, *Have we done anything wrong?* When they shook their heads, she turned slowly back to stare at the captain. He walked with his head down, like a conquered man, and stood by the mizzenmast for a long time without speaking. When he finally lifted his eyes to speak, his voice rumbled with weariness.

"We are lost," he said, after clearing his throat. "I know not how much longer we can stay in this fog. Our provisions won't last the rest of the voyage if we stay put much longer, and if the wind blew, we would not dare move at any great speed because we do not know in what direction we are going. In truth, this fog has made steering impossible."

"Can't we just raise all the sails and try to move out of it as fast as we can?" Thatcher asked.

Captain Blade gave him a weary smile. "There is no wind to speak of," he said. "Not enough to fill even a topgallant. Nothing moves this heavy cloud from us. 'Tis almost as if we are held prisoner here, and only the hand of God shall release us." He paused and leaned back upon the stout pole of the mizzenmast. "I've been praying—though I don't know why God should have cause to hear my prayers—and I have come to ask that you pray, too. My men are convinced that God has his hand on us, and I've heard the Almighty has a special ear for the prayers of children. So if ye will pray—"

He stopped abruptly, as if an urgent emotion had choked his voice, and Kimberly felt her heart swell with sympathy for the stern captain. She had seen him angry, confident, proud, and contented, but even when he had been staring down the twin cannons of a pirate who planned to sink their ship, she had never seen him defeated. Until now.

"Captain Blade." A voice broke the stillness in the room, and Kimberly's heart began to beat faster when Ethan stood and walked to the captain. She knew he was upset and depressed. What on earth was he going to say?

"Captain Blade, are you familiar with the story of Jonah?"

A weary smile crossed the captain's face as he looked at Ethan. "Yea, son, I am. What of it?"

"Jonah was disobeying the God of Israel, so the Master of the universe sent a storm that threatened an entire ship. 'Twas only when Jonah surrendered that the ship was released from the storm."

The captain drew his lips into a thin line. "Are you saying that we have a Jonah aboard? A sinner?"

"Yea," Ethan answered, looking down at the floor. "And 'tis me."

"You?" Captain Blade bent at the waist and leaned toward Ethan, resting his hands on his knees. "I've been

156

watching you, and you're a good lad. What could you have done for God to punish you with such a severe hand?"

Ethan's face grew red under the concentrated stares of the captain and the other watching children. "I have not kept the Law of my people. I have not been a good Jew."

Kimberly thought the captain might laugh, but he merely ran his hand over his bearded chin as if he were deep in thought. "We need the blessing of God on this ship," Captain Blade said finally. "And 'twould do all of us good to lift our thoughts heavenward and beseech the aid of the Almighty. What can we do to help you walk more closely with your God?"

Ethan looked up at Kimberly for a moment, his eyes dark and pleading.

"We could pray," she suggested, stepping forward. "Ethan could pray in his way, and we in ours, and together we could beg God for deliverance from this dark cloud."

"Aye, your prayers would of certain work something," Captain Blade said, straightening his shoulders. He glanced around the room, then turned his dark eyes toward Kimberly. "Pray if you will, Miss Hollis, and may God grant your petitions. I'm hoping he does, or else we will all perish here in this godforsaken sea."

157

Looks of mingled awe and fear followed the captain as he moved away and lifted the hatch that led to the lower hold. When he had gone, Brooke broke the silence by asking for volunteers to pray. She glanced pointedly at Kimberly, but Kimberly ignored Brooke and walked toward the companionway that led to the lower deck. She had been wondering about something for a very long time, and now was as good a time as any to gather her courage and find her answer.

* * *

"Captain Blade?" He was standing with the bilge boys near the fire that burned atop a thick pile of sand on the floor. At the sound of her voice the captain turned and looked at Kimberly.

"What do you want?" he asked, not unpleasantly. "Is there trouble above?"

"Nay," she answered, stepping closer. "'Tis you I've come about."

"Me?" He smiled then, a heart-stopping smile that made her want to blush and stamp her foot at the same time because she knew he was laughing at her. Did he think her only a foolish child?

"Yea, about you," she answered, strengthening her voice. "You've said more than once that you do not think God will answer your prayers."

"Aye, you've heard me correctly. Why should God hear the prayers of one such as I?"

"The Bible says God hears the fervent prayers of a righteous man." She pointed toward the trapdoor above her head. "We wrote that verse down on our parchment, and if you'd like I'll show it to you."

"There's no need," the captain answered. He turned and murmured directions to the three bilge boys, then moved away from them and sank onto the top of a barrel. He crossed his arms and scratched his chin as he studied her. "Why care you for my soul, Kimberly Hollis? Why do you dare to risk my displeasure by coming here alone to ask me this question?"

"A true Christian cares for the soul of every man and woman," she said, feeling a hot blush burn her cheeks.

"Even a ruffian such as I?"

"My mother didn't think you were a ruffian. Before she died, she said that you were a kind man. And I'll never forget that you were gentle with her—even at the end."

The captain closed his eyes and nodded at the

158

memory, then the lines of his face hardened. "But kindness does not a Christian make. Even your friend Ethan is kind, from what I've seen, and he does not call himself a Christian."

"Ethan is searching. He is not happy."

"And I am not happy, either. And so you are taking it upon yourself to save our souls."

Kimberly sighed in exasperation, feeling as though the room had spun around. A moment ago she had been confidently in control of the situation. She had come below to help the captain, to ask why he felt himself out of God's favor, and then assure him that no one need ever worry that God would not forgive. But now the captain was asking questions for which she had no answer.

She spread her hands in the air. "I just wanted to know why you think God will not hear you."

Captain Blade laughed. "How can you ask such a thing? You see me on this ship, with these captive children, and yet you think God will hear my prayers? You were not aboard, Miss Hollis, when first they began to arrive. They cried for their mamas and papas, they wept, they tore their hair and sobbed most piteously all through the day and night. And yet more and more children came, brought by men the likes of which I'd never seen before, and I turned my back and closed my eyes as little ones were pitched, screaming and fighting, into the hold where you so peaceably pass your days. Youngsters scarcely five years old were brought aboard, and two wee ones died before we even left London. I do thank God that the others were spared that pitiful sight."

Kimberly shivered with a cold that was not from the air. The mocking light had gone from the captain's eyes, and his face was stiff with the horror of his memories. "I shudder now to think what I have done. And I know that God will not forgive me, at least not while I have these poor kidnapped children aboard my ship. I sold my honor

159

for a vessel of wood and canvas, Miss Hollis, and I don't think you can understand that."

"You didn't take the children," Kimberly whispered.

"Nay," Blade said, pressing his hand to his forehead as he gazed wearily around the cargo hold. "But I didn't stop those who did. There's a man in London—a man of power and authority—who has invested heavily in a plantation at Jamestown. He needs hands to work the tobacco fields, and 'twas he who arranged the capture of these youngsters. He told me to think of the children as cargo, only cargo, so I agreed to command the vessel. In return he agreed that upon my arrival at Jamestown, the *Seven Brothers* would be mine."

He looked at her again, his eyes large and fierce with pain. "I was a captain without a ship, Miss Kimberly, and I don't expect that you'd be knowing what that's like."

"I would imagine," Kimberly whispered, choosing her words carefully, "that 'tis a bit like being a child without a mother." Her words cut him, for he actually cringed as she spoke, then the captain lowered his head. "But you don't have to worry," she went on, "for God has brought us together as a family. The children living above are doing well, and many came aboard willingly and look forward to a new life in Virginia. And no matter what you may think, Captain, God can and will forgive. He will accept you when you are ready to turn to him."

Was that a flicker of interest in those dark eyes, or was he now listening only to amuse himself? Kimberly didn't know, for at that moment the other seamen dropped through the companionway and began to line up for dinner.

But as Captain Blade stood to make room for his approaching men, he turned again to Kimberly. "Thank you for your concern," he said, his voice warm and sincere. "And if your prayers get us out of this infernal fog, mayhap I'll believe that God remains on speaking terms with me."

160

Tuesday, June 8

21

Captain Blade had asked the children to pray for wind. The next day those prayers were answered.

Bawling winds that did nothing more than churn the seas and move the dark mist from one place to another began to hoot through the children's hold. The threatening fog that had surrounded the ship darkened into a mass of black, boiling clouds. By midday, lightning regularly cracked the gray skies apart, and rain began to fall after dinner. The raindrops, sharp as needles through the open windows, drove the children against the walls of the ship.

The rain fell into darkly reflecting mirrors of puddles on the glistening wood planks, and Kimberly caught a glance of her own tense face in the water. *How much longer will this continue?* she wondered, taking pains to smooth her expression so the younger ones wouldn't see her concern. *'Tis bad enough to endure a squall at sea, but to face a churning storm after a week of dense fog . . .*

Caught up in the claws of the wind, the ship climbed one creaming slope of a mountainous wave, then slipped over its roaring top before beginning the journey again. Overhead, Kimberly could hear the muffled cries of the seamen as they worked to batten down the hatches and secure the ship's cannon. Once, the sharp sounds of cracking wood, rolling thunder, and a man's scream made Kimberly shiver. "Sounds like a cannon broke loose," Thatcher explained when she looked his way. "Probably ran over a sailor's foot."

The sea outside spat up in white plumes, a frightful contrast to the gray mass that hovered over the water and curtained off the sky. Did the blue sky even exist anymore? Kimberly hadn't seen it in days, and she wondered if the world had shifted its course somehow. If the sun had burnt itself out and died, wouldn't the sea behave strangely? Maybe spring no longer led to summer, and summer wouldn't lead to autumn, or autumn to winter.

A lump rose in her throat. Such a reversal was unthinkable. God had put the earth into motion and decreed the seasons and times of the moon and sea. He wouldn't forsake his creation. And he wouldn't forsake her.

162   Instinctively, she reached into her pocket and pulled out the verse-scrawled parchment. Her words of God. The only words that could bring comfort during a storm like this.

" 'What time I am afraid, I will trust in thee,'" she began to read, unfolding the page. She strengthened her voice so that all might hear. "'I will say of the Lord, He is my refuge and my fortress: my God; in him will I trust. He shall cover thee with his feathers, and under his wings shalt thou trust: his truth shall be thy shield and buckler.'"

The children around her began to quiet their weeping.

"'Thou shalt not be afraid for the terror by night;

nor for the arrow that flieth by day. For he shall give his angels charge over thee, to keep thee in all thy ways. They shall bear thee up in their hands, lest thou dash thy foot against a stone.'"

A sudden spattering of raindrops hit the page, blurring the ink, and Kimberly tried to smooth the paper against her kirtle to wipe the water from the parchment.

"'The Lord is thy keeper,'" she read, "'the Lord is thy shade upon thy right hand. The Lord shall preserve thy going out and thy coming in from this time forth, and even for evermore—'"

A sharp gust of wind tore the page from Kimberly's hands. She scrambled forward to stop it, but the parchment danced away in the breath of the wind. "Oh, help me catch it," she cried, nearly knocking over a huddle of children as she pressed past them to reach the windblown page. "Don't just sit there! Help me catch our words of God!"

She dove and ran, but the frightful wind held the parchment just out of the reach of her fingertips, as though it were teasing her. The other children didn't budge from their secure positions as the ship bucked and pitched in the storm.

"Forget it, Kimberly," Brooke called from the corner where she sat with Abigail and Christian. "Grab on to something, or you're going to hurt yourself!"

"I can't let it go," Kimberly screamed into the wind. She made another desperate dive for the parchment as it hovered near the center of the ship. Just as Kimberly threw herself upon it, a wayward gust of air blew the parchment away from her hand. Propelled by momentum and the rocking of the ship, Kimberly fell forward and solidly hit her head on the mainmast.

"Ouch," she said, rubbing her head as she sat up. Dazed and sore, she watched with disbelieving eyes as the airborne parchment flew out the window, lingered for a moment as if to say good-bye, then vanished into the rain and wind. "'Tis gone."

"Let it go," Thatcher called. He crawled forward from the relative shelter of the walls and pulled Kimberly out of the open space in the center of the hold. "You're soaking wet, Kimberly," he said, gently teasing her. "Don't you have enough sense to come out of the rain?"

The other children's faces seemed to swim for a moment beneath Kimberly's eyes, then a flush of anger brought things into focus. "Why didn't you help me?" she yelled at Thatcher, glaring at him with all the strength she could muster.

"We're in a storm, dearie," he said, pulling her toward him as though she were a stubborn child. "Come over here where 'tis dry."

"Nay! I won't," Kimberly said, yanking her hands away from him. Reeling on the uneven and unpredictable deck of the ship, she staggered to the center of the hold and supported herself on the stem of the mainmast. Narrowing her eyes, she pointed a shaky finger toward the others who lined the walls. "You all ought to be ashamed of yourselves," she said, screaming to be heard above the bawling winds. "We had but a few Scriptures, and they've just flown out the window. And not a one of you bothered to help me catch them."

Ashamed and quiet, the other children turned their faces from her. Kimberly whirled around in the rain, and when no one would listen or look at her, she staggered toward the door that would take her to the lower hold. Maybe there she could find enough peace and quiet to apologize to God for losing his words. She certainly didn't want to pray with the others. They didn't care.

* * *

Ethan watched the storm with wide eyes as two voices in his brain argued with one another. *'Tis a judgment of God, for he is displeased with you,* one voice said. The other answered, *'Tis just a storm, just as the blue light upon the mainmast was just lightning. You think too much, Ethan Reis. You have taken a dream much too seriously.*

Was it only a dream? His father had looked at him with eyes of fire and said, "These vapors of chaos and unrest will not leave until you assume your rightful place in this world." And on that day the ship had become lost in the fog. Was it mere coincidence? Or part of God's plan?

He was a Jew, that much he could not doubt. He would never be an ordinary boy. His heritage and responsibilities were too deeply ingrained to be ignored. He was a child of Abraham, a son of those who had journeyed to Egypt and toiled under the taskmaster pharaohs. He was a descendant of those who had come out of Egypt by God's grace and by the blood of the Passover lamb.

He had always felt especially close to his people during the Passover Seder. Whenever he ate the customary feast with his family, thousands of years of tradition had encircled him in his home, uniting him with Jews of the past, present, and future in an unbroken chain. Since the beginning in Egypt so many years ago, Jews had been celebrating feasts of the Passover. This was one of the things that made the Jews a distinctive people.

Ethan stood from the place where he had been sitting and walked unsteadily to the open space in the center of the hold. He could feel the curious eyes of the others upon him, but he did not care. Though it was summer and not spring, though he was on a ship and not at home, though he was alone and not with his family, Ethan Reis was going to celebrate a Passover Seder.

Quietly and reverently, he bowed his head. "The woman of the house comes first," he said, talking to no one in particular. "She lights the Passover candles and

165

sings the blessing to begin the meal. Thus it has always been, and thus it will always be."

Closing his eyes, Ethan lifted his hands and began to hum the blessing.

* * *

Below in the bilge boys' hold, Kimberly fell to her knees and lifted her eyes to the ceiling above. "Father God," she prayed, swaying as the ship tossed and casks shifted position around her, "I am sorry that your words slipped out of my hands. The others wouldn't help, Lord, and I don't know what you'll want to do about that. But I worked so hard and risked a great deal to go to the captain. So why did you allow this storm to steal your words? 'Twould seem to me that you would want us to have a few Scriptures to think about while we're here—"

"Excuse me, miss?"

Kimberly opened her eyes and saw one of the bilge boys standing next to her. She recognized him; he was called Locke. Locke's face was even paler than usual, and slightly green. "What is it, Locke?"

"Is the ship going down? Is that why you're praying?"

"Nay," she said, managing an impatient smile. "The ship is fine, I'm certain. We've weathered a worse storm than this, don't you remember? And Captain Blade is a fine pilot. He'll bring us through."

"Then why"—Locke crinkled his face in a puzzled expression—"if all is well, why are you praying?"

"Oh," Kimberly explained, feeling suddenly embarrassed. "I don't know if you'll understand. I had written out a few verses from the Bible on a sheet of parchment, and the wind blew the paper out the window. But I had worked hard to gather those verses, for no one above has a Bible, you see. Though the captain has his prayer book 'tis not the same as the Bible—"

"Do you mean this?" Locke reached into the waistband of his dirty breeches and pulled out a small brown book. Though the cover was tattered and torn, Kimberly could clearly read: *Holy Bible.*

"Merciful heavens!" she gasped, scarcely daring to believe what she saw. "Why, I never knew you had one down here!"

"I didn't tell you about it when you asked," Locke answered, grinning sheepishly. "But you can have it now. None of us bilge rats can read."

"If you can't read, why do you keep it?" Kimberly asked, running one finger over the cover as he held it out to her.

Locke shrugged. "For good luck, I suppose. For the protection of God."

Kimberly gave him a thoughtful smile. "I don't suppose you'd be willing to let me teach you how to read?"

"I will, if you will read the Bible to me," he answered, shyly hanging his head. "I've been wondering what it could say to make you want it so badly."

"It says wonderful things," Kimberly said. "And I'll do better than just read to you. I'll ask the captain if you can come up every morning. I'm teaching the young ones to read, and I can teach you, too."

"Could you now?" Locke asked, honest excitement in his eyes.

"And me?" another boy asked.

"And me, too?" the third boy called.

"Yea," Kimberly said, taking the Bible Locke offered. She hugged it to her chest. "We'll begin on the morrow, or as soon as this storm passes. I promise."

A sudden thumping noise overhead jerked all of their eyes toward the ceiling, and Kimberly was surprised to see Wingate's face appear in the companionway opening. "Kimberly, come quick!" he yelled as rain poured off his face and shoulders. "Ethan's not right! You've got to come now!"

167

"What do you mean, he's not right?" Kimberly asked as she scrambled toward the ladder.

"He's out of his head," Wingate answered. "He's out of his right mind!"

* * *

"We purge the leaven out of the house," Ethan explained as the other children watched him with wide, curious eyes. Behind him, he heard footsteps on the companion ladder and knew that Kimberly had been called up from the cargo hold. Undoubtedly she would think him crazy, too.

Thunder rolled through the heavens, and Ethan ignored it. "All of the leaven must go," he went on, not caring what anyone thought of him. "My father makes a game of it. After my mother cleans the kitchen, my father sprinkles a few bread crumbs through the house and bids my sister and me to find them. When we do, he takes a feather and sweeps them into a wooden spoon, then casts the crumbs into the fire."

"Why does he do that?"

Ethan turned. Kimberly stood directly behind him, her hair blowing in the storm, her face wet with rain. But her manner and her words were as calm as if she were out for a stroll in the park on Sunday afternoon.

"Why, to cleanse the house of sin, of course," Ethan answered, knowing full well that she was trying to humor him. "Leaven represents sin, and we are to purge our houses and our lives before the Passover Seder. That's what I'm trying to do now. I want to be a good Jew."

"I know you do, Ethan," Kimberly answered, coming closer. She stood next to him and pointed toward the empty space in the center of the hold. "If this were your house, what would your family do next?"

Ethan felt some of the chilliness leave his heart, and he gave Kimberly a warm smile. Perhaps she did understand. "At sundown on the first full moon of spring, my mother would light the Passover candles. She brings the light to the table and sings the blessing."

Ethan lifted his hands and sang the gentle melody just as his mother had: "Blessed are you, O Lord our God, King of the universe, who sanctifies us by your commandments and has ordained that we kindle the Passover lights."

Kimberly nodded as if she were picturing the scene. "What then?"

"Then my father pours the first cup of wine—the cup of sanctification. He looks over the table to see that everything is perfectly in place, that all is right for the Passover meal. When he knows everything is ready, he drinks from the first cup and takes up three pieces of *matzo*."

"What is matzo?" Kimberly called through the noise of the wind. "I've never seen it."

"'Tis an unleavened bread," Ethan explained slowly. "Thin, and grilled so there are stripes which run along its surface. The bakers poke holes into it so that it will cook through."

"I see," Kimberly whispered, a thoughtful look upon her face.

"While we watch, my father takes a special cloth bag, beautifully embroidered, and prepares to place the three pieces of matzo into the bag's three special compartments. But before he does, the second piece of matzo is broken, and half of it is wrapped in white linen and hidden away while my sister and I cover our eyes. The hidden piece is called the *Afikomen*."

"How unusual," Kimberly murmured.

Ethan lowered his voice. "Then my father always turns to my sister, the youngest, and she asks the four questions about why this night is different from all others. My sister asks why we only eat matzo on this

169

night, why we eat bitter vegetables, why we dip our vegetables in salt water, and why we recline as we eat. My father answers that we were once slaves in Egypt, but now we are free, so we set aside this night to remember the great things God has done for us. We eat unleavened bread because our fathers had no time to wait for yeast bread to rise before fleeing the slavery of Egypt. The salt water and bitter herbs remind us of the tears we shed while in bondage. And we recline to express the rest we enjoy as free people."

A sudden gust of rain-filled wind blew through the hold, causing the other children to squeal and cower again against the wall, but Ethan ignored it, so caught up was he in his memories. "Then my father holds up the lamb bone to remind us of the lamb that was killed on that first Passover. The blood was spread on the doorposts and lintel of the house to protect the home from the tenth plague. God passed over us when he saw the blood."

"I think I understand," Kimberly said, her eyes following Ethan's hand as he wiped the top and two sides of an imaginary door.

Ethan then held up an invisible goblet. "Next my father takes his cup and spills it ten times, once for each of the ten plagues in Egypt. After that, each person in my family places a bit of horseradish on a matzo and eats it, symbolizing the bitterness of Israel's slavery. Then we place *charoseth*—a mixture of apples, nuts, honey, and cinnamon—upon the matzo and eat it, too, as a reminder of the mortar that the people of Israel used to make bricks."

Ethan paused for a moment. It was at this point that his family began to eat their meal, a rich feast that his mother worked hard to prepare. But here aboard the *Seven Brothers* there was little to feast upon. The supply of meat had nearly been exhausted, and the hardtack was too much like unleavened bread to be a treat.

"Then, we eat," he said, knowing his disappointment

was evident on his face. What had he expected to accomplish by explaining this precious ritual to the Gentiles around him? Only Kimberly seemed to care about what he was describing. The others looked at him as if he were absolutely mad. And though he had clearly seen the beloved faces of his family in his imagination, replaying the ritual had done nothing to ease his loneliness.

"Tell us what you're eating," Brooke called from the crowd. Ethan jerked his head toward her. She huddled with the others, out of the rain, but her eyes shone with genuine interest. Was she making fun of him?

"We are eating nothing," he said, waving his hand toward the empty space. "There is nothing here."

Kimberly stepped forward and slipped her hand about his waist. "Mayhap the Lord will provide a feast," she said, wiping a strand of wet hair from her forehead. "Did he not feed the children of Israel while they wandered in the wilderness?"

Ethan was about to protest that manna had fallen generations ago and not since, but a sudden commotion from above distracted him. Irregular thumping noises came from the deck above, and he could hear the muffled cries of seamen.

"What is happening up there?" he asked aloud, but the wind shifted and the ship listed to one side so violently that he and Kimberly slid and slipped across the floor. The younger ones screamed. Kimberly yelled orders while Thatcher scrambled to help. The slanting rain came forcefully through the open windows, and in the rain Ethan found the reason for the seamen's cries of confusion: Fish had begun to fall from the sky.

22

As the ship leaned at a dangerous angle, rain poured directly through the open windows, and Kimberly heard the smack of objects falling around her. Her heart began to pound when something fell through the rain and hit her on the head. Brooke was screaming, the young ones were crying, and Wingate flailed his arms hysterically as he slid across the floor. Abigail was leaning against the wall of the ship, her face deathly pale, while all around on the floor small fish flopped in puddles of rain. Glancing out the window, Kimberly could see that fish were falling from the sky with such force that they actually bounced when they hit the water.

"Merciful heavens," Kimberly whispered, staring at the unbelievable sight. "What has brought this upon us?"

Suddenly an ear-shattering scream cut through the confusion, and Kimberly whirled around to see Brooke slide across the floor, half blind with unreasoning terror.

A long, black eel had wrapped itself around her neck, and Brooke was frozen in horror and powerless to remove it. As Kimberly watched in amazement, Thatcher sprang toward Brooke, grasped the creature in his hands, and flung it out the window. Brooke curled into a frightened huddle at Kimberly's feet.

The fish fall lasted only for a moment more. As the boat righted itself to an even keel, the skies seemed to calm, and the rain fell in a steady stream. In puddles, on the floor, and on the girls' kirtles and the boys' breeches, an odd assortment of fish flopped and writhed.

"How disgusting!" Brooke cried, wiping tears from her eyes. "I've never been so frightened in my life! What happened? I've never heard of such a thing! 'Tis not natural!"

"Waterspouts," Thatcher said, kicking a spiny blowfish out of his way. "The seamen told me about them. Waterspouts pick the fish up and drop them elsewhere." He slipped out of his shirt and gathered the fabric like a sack in his hand. "Maybe 'tis not natural, but 'tis welcome." He stooped and began to gather the fish. "And you were just saying, Kimberly, that the Lord would provide the feast! Fish are better than dried beef jerky, I'll warrant!"

174

Kimberly opened her mouth in surprise as she remembered her words. She looked around the hold for Ethan and found him sitting by the mainmast, his arm propped on one raised knee.

He looked at her with a dazed expression when she crawled over to him. "See, Ethan, what has happened! I told you the Lord would provide your feast! Now we'll have fish to eat on the morrow, or mayhap even tonight!"

"I don't understand," Ethan said slowly. "I didn't think anything would happen."

"So, you have a Passover feast now," Kimberly said, leaning on her elbow. She ignored the squeals and screams of the others as they gathered the sea creatures. Ethan's eyes were still troubled, and she knew the reason for his sorrow went far deeper than the storm and the freakish fish fall. "Go on, Ethan, and tell me about Passover. What happens next? You weren't finished, were you?"

"Nay," Ethan said, still dazed. He paused a moment, then seemed to find his thoughts. "After my family eats dinner, my father tells us to hunt for the hidden matzo— the Afikomen. Whoever finds it earns a reward, mayhap a coin or a piece of candy. Then we break the Afikomen into pieces and share it, and my father blesses it by saying, 'Blessed are you, O Lord our God, King of the universe, who bringest forth bread from the earth.' And so we eat the matzo and drink the third cup that my father had blessed."

Ethan paused again as if his thoughts had wandered far away. Kimberly urged him forward: "And what then, Ethan?"

"Then my father sends us to the door to see if Elijah has come," he said. "It has been said that Elijah will prepare the way for the Messiah, so we look for him to bring our coming king. Finally, my father lifts the fourth cup, the cup of praise, and quotes the Scriptures: 'And I will take you to me for a people, and I will be to you a God: and ye shall know that I am the Lord your God, which bringeth you out from under the burdens of the Egyptians.'

"And then," Ethan said, his voice choking with emotion, "my father lifts his cup and says to us, 'Next year in Jerusalem!'" He paused for a moment, lifting his own hand high, and his eyes clouded with sadness. "But I will not eat the Passover with my family in Jerusalem or anywhere else. My family is lost to me. I fear my faith is lost, too."

"Nay, say not so!" Kimberly said, leaning toward

175

him. "Do you not see the picture, Ethan? Think back with me. Your father leads the Seder, does he not?"

"Yea," Ethan nodded. "'Tis the father's role, for he is the head of the home."

"Yea, but 'tis the woman who brings the light to the table and begins the ceremony," Kimberly pointed out. "Just as the Scriptures prophesied that a woman would bring the Light of the World from God. Know you who this woman was?"

"I know who she will be," Ethan answered. "Isaiah told us, 'Behold, a virgin shall conceive, and bear a son, and shall call his name Immanuel.'"

"Yea, and that virgin was Mary," Kimberly whispered. "'Twas she who brought the Light of the World to us. And the matzo—the way you described it reminded me of something. You said 'twas striped, and pierced, and without leaven."

Ethan seemed to stumble through his thoughts. "Isaiah again," he said. "He said the Messiah would be wounded for our transgressions, bruised for our iniquities, and with his stripes we are healed."

"Yea," Kimberly said, flipping through the Bible in her hand. After a moment, she laid her finger on the passage in Isaiah and continued to read: "'He was numbered with the transgressors; and he bare the sin of many.'" She glanced up at Ethan. "Just as the Passover lamb had to die so that its blood would cause the angel of death to pass over the Israelites in Egypt, even so the Messiah had to die so that his blood could purge our sins."

"Nay," Ethan said, shaking his head. "The Messiah has not yet come!"

"The broken and hidden matzo," Kimberly said, trying to catch his eyes. "'Twas hidden away from sight, then your family rejoiced when 'twas found and eaten. On the night Jesus was betrayed, Ethan, he ate Passover with his followers and told them that the bread, the unleavened

176

matzo, was his body that was to be broken for them. He was pierced, Ethan, with a spear, and whipped with the stripes of a lash. He was without sin, just as the matzo is without leaven. His body was hidden away for three days, but then he rose again."

"A fable," Ethan said, throwing up his hands. "A Gentile fable."

"Nay," Kimberly said, gently closing the Bible in her lap. "You yourself told me the blessing: Blessed are you, O Lord, King of the universe, who *bringest forth bread from the earth*. Jesus was born in Bethlehem as the prophets foretold. He is the Bread of Life, Ethan, and God brought him forth from the earth after three days."

Ethan closed his eyes. Confusion and fear were written upon his face.

"John the Baptist once baptized Jews who were awaiting the coming Messiah," Kimberly said. "When John saw Jesus coming toward him he called out, 'Behold the Lamb of God, which taketh away the sin of the world.' The Jews who heard him *knew* what he meant. Jesus is the Passover lamb, slain once and for all men."

She softened her smile. "Ethan, God has provided answers for those who hunger and thirst for his truth. I am praying you will find them."

177

* * *

Within an hour the storm abated, the wind ceased, and the fog bank withdrew until it was nothing more than a memory. Blue sky appeared overhead again, reaching out and over across the sea. The sails of the *Seven Brothers* cracked and bellied taut in the wind as the ship moved at a stately pace through the water. Relief like a visible wave passed over the crew and the captives, and the air in the hold steamed with the delicious aroma of the fish stew simmering in the lower hold.

If not for her wet clothes and the bump on her head

from crashing into the mast, Kimberly could almost have believed that the entire week had been a terrible dream. But every terrifying moment—the fog, the storm, the fish fall—had been real.

Kimberly wondered what Ethan would think now that the fog had lifted. He had seemed to believe that the mist was some sort of punishment intended for him, so what would he think now that the skies were clear?

She did not have to wait long to discover her answer. She found Ethan sitting by the window, his eyes fastened to the pages of the precious Bible Locke had given her. She was surprised that Ethan would willingly read the Bible—it was, after all, complete with the Old and New Testaments. But he read rapidly and silently, his finger flitting over the pages as he mouthed the words.

At last, when her shadow fell across the page, he looked up. His eyes were alight with a look she'd never seen in them before. "I have a verse for you, Kimberly," he said, a smile warming his face. "'Tis found in Proverbs."

Her eyes swept his face for a clue to his thoughts, but she could find nothing in his eyes but confident joy. "Let's hear it, then," she said, settling down beside him. "I've always had a fancy for the Proverbs."

Ethan concentrated on the page before him. "'Who hath ascended up into heaven or descended?'" he read. "'Who hath gathered the wind in his fists? who hath bound the waters in a garment? who hath established all the ends of the earth? what is his name, and what is his son's name, if thou canst tell?'"

"Well?" Kimberly said, waiting.

"His name is Jehovah, Master of the universe," Ethan said, his eyes boring into hers. "And his son's name is Joshua!"

"Joshua?" Kimberly asked, worried. She lifted an eyebrow. "Ethan, what have you been reading?"

178

He threw back his head and laughed. "Joshua means *Yeshua*, his Hebrew name. I think you know him by the Greek name *Jesus*."

"Yea, I do," Kimberly said, smiling. "Indeed I do know him."